Rebecca Brown

THE CHILDREN'S CRUSADE

3/14/91.

for Gloria

from Rebecca Brown

The Seal Press

This United States paperback edition first published in 1991 by
The Seal Press, 3131 Western Avenue, Suite 410, Seattle,
Washington 98121.

Part of this book first appeared in a different form as 'Das
letzte Mal, daβ ich und die Chuck die Richs besuchten' in
Sweet Little Sixteen (Fugend in den USA) ed. Juergen Schoeneich,
Rowohlt Taschenbuch Verlag GMBH.

Cover art by Margaret Chodos-Irvine.

Library of Congress Cataloging-in-Publication Data

Brown, Rebecca, 1956-
    The children's crusade / Rebecca Brown.
        p.   cm.
    ISBN 1-878087-04-4 :
    I. Title.
PS3552.R6973C4   1991
813'.54--dc20   90-20008
                                                        CIP

Printed in the United States of America.
First printing, March 1991
10 9 8 7 6 5 4 3 2 1

Foreign Distribution:
In Canada: Raincoast Book Distribution, Vancouver, B.C.
In Great Britain and Europe: Airlift Book Company, London
In Australia: Stilone, N.S.W.

1

The Cold War

I

Everything outside is white. Everything outside is clean and covered.

I am in the living room wearing fuzzy blue socks and sitting on one of the two beige-covered, hard-soft chairs with the high backs. They used to be our grandmother's but she gave them to us and my mother had them re-upholstered. They're soft because they have cushions that cover most of them except the skinny dark wooden legs, the two-inch ends of arms, and a frame strip around the top. I can only reach that if I turn around, kneel up on the seat and stretch. But they're hard because the cushions are so tight and hard. In our grandparents' house no one sat on them, but we do at home.

I move over to the tall front window. I see my brother Stan outside. Cold comes up through my socks where the carpet stops just before the beige radiator. The top of my right foot is warm from it. I rub a circle in the steamy glass with the side of my fist and I see my brother and his friend Tommy playing. They're lying on their backs swishing their arms up and down by their sides. When they jump up, they wipe the snow from each other's backs. I don't hear most of what they say, but I hear them call the shapes they've pressed down in it angel wings.

My brother and Tommy squat behind a wall of solid white in our yard, right next to the street. Stuck into the wall is a stick. My brother's cap hangs from it like a flag. Across the street our neighbours' kids have also built a wall. They're making balls and throwing them at each other. The balls break into little white sprays when they hit, but sometimes before they hit, just in the air. Stan and Tommy crawl around sweeping it to themselves with their arms and making balls. They put them into piles. My brother and Tommy tell each other to hurry. They throw handfuls of it at each other and laugh. Stan fists it, plays it back and forth between one hand and the other. He packs it hard and adds a little more. He's fast. My brother puts smaller rows on top of the bottom rows in a pyramid. He's careful when he puts them in the pyramid because if they're not hard enough, they break in his hands. My brother and the kids across the street yell something, then throw them at each other. They crouch down behind the wall and giggle while they gather up more to throw.

'Honey—' I turn from the window. My mother's calling me. She stands on the first step to the upstairs on the light brown carpet, just a little darker than the hard-soft chairs. She holds a bundle of clothes over her left arm. Her right hand holds a small pair of black galoshes. I rush to her. 'Wanna go out and play with Stan?'

'Out there?' I look up at her.

'In the cold you mean? Sure, it's OK. I'll bundle you up.'

We sit down beside each other on the first step. She drops the clothes in her lap. She holds a sock and puts her arm around me. I stick my left foot out, grab on to her for support, and twist into the second layer of sock. We repeat this with my right foot, only this time I help hold the sock. Putting one sock on over the other, my mother explains how layers keep you warm. I put one leg in an old pair of my brother's trousers. My mother pulls the legs up so my feet come out, then I stand up and she and I pull them up. I stick my hands in the deep pockets. She tucks my shirt in then snaps them tight. She picks up the galoshes and motions me back to the step. She takes one of the galoshes in her hand and puts her arm around me. I stick my toes in. She pulls the boot and I push the foot. I stomp on the floor, pushing the boot all the way on. Same with the other boot. I sit down and my mother fastens the black metal clips up the front of the rubbery galoshes.

My mother picks up a sweater by the shoulders. I throw my hands up in the air, fists clenched, and close my eyes. My mother slips my glasses off. I giggle and open my eyes. My mother is fuzzy like my brother was outside before I cleaned the spot in the window with my fist. My mother is a peach-coloured circle with dark around the top. My mother places the neck of the sweater over me, gently pulls the bottom down all around. I feel her hand searching for mine

4

through the open sleeve of left, then right, upstretched arm. She squashes the sleeves down over my hands. I unclench my fist and flex my fingers to wave. 'Hello-o-o,' she answers. The sound is muffled by the sweater still over my head. I feel her hands down by the bottom and on the collar. She holds the collar forward so it's not too tight on my face when she pulls it down. I blink and smile. 'Hello there,' she says. She's blurred. Some of my hair has fallen in front of my eyes. She smooths my hair out of my face and hands me my glasses. When I put them on, she fuzzes back to focus.

My mittens are big and fat. On the inside they feel like a kitten's fur. I take my thumb in and out of the mitten thumb. She fastens them to my sweater with the small silver clips that dangle from the wrists by yarn.

My mother goes to the hall closet. She holds my winter coat for me and helps me put my arms in. She crouches down in front of me to do the buttons. Her soft fast hands secure me in. She tucks a scarf around my neck. She's right down beside me. She leans to me and I look into her hair. Her face is almost by mine. I look down at her, but maybe it only seems that way. Maybe she and I are even, but it seems like she's down below me because I'm so used to looking up at her. I can smell her skin. She smells like soap and breakfast. She smells like toast and coffee and eggs and that pink soap with the lady in the circle on it. I can feel how warm she is just there right down beside me. Her skin is so close and soft and she says. 'There you go—'

I've almost forgotten what we're doing. But I'm all dressed and I say, 'Thank you Momma.' I wish we weren't finished. I say, 'Momma—'

She's stood up so quickly, before I can even say it again, 'Momma—' I wish she hadn't. I liked her down there. I wanted to tell her something, when she was right there with her hands on the shiny brown buttons and I could see her hair right there. But now she's stood up. Her hands are going for the closet again.

'Momma—'

'Mmmm?'

She's turned almost completely to the closet. I see her back and I'm looking up at her. Does she think I'm going to say nothing? Like 'Oh great,' or 'Will Stan watch me?' or 'Could I stay out for a long time?', when I say 'Momma—' and she says, 'Mmmm?'

I can see the colours of everything. Momma's slacks are brown wool. I can see each thread and hair in the wool. I can see the way it's woven. It looks like Vs going one way and then Vs going the other way. There's teeny dots of black and dark brown and Indian brown

5

and orange-brown and grey-black and white and tiny hairs that go out at the edges. Every time she moves a little bit, the edge changes, but every edge has little teeny hairs. She has on white stretchy anklets, and grey-brown hush puppies, soft to look at, with the hush-puppy stuff worn down at the toe. Her soles are skinny and black and flat and I can see the brown colour of the thread where the shoes are sewn like Xs and the shoelaces are chocolate. Her dark suede vest is darker than chocolate, like coffee. She drinks coffee a lot and her white blouse comes out of her vest and her hands come out of her shirt and her hands and her arms stretch over to the closet.

'Momma—'

'Mmmm?'

Her hands are brown and they feel like soft, soft leather, only warm. Her hands stretch out towards the top shelf on the closet. Her fingernails are cut medium length, not painted, but white and clean. On the fourth finger on her left hand, the fingernail is curved under from when she was little. There are little white moons on each of her fingernails right where they come out of the finger. There's a skinny line of skin between the real skin and the nail. The soft cracks in her flesh are triangle shapes over her knuckles. Her hand stretches up. The loose flesh over the straightened joints looks like circles with stripes. Her hands are clean and pink and brown and separate from everything. I can see faint blue lines of veins.

'Momma—'

I hear the syllables knock themselves against themselves. I hear them say themselves again, slowly. It takes a long time, as long as it takes the ground to get completely white. My lips touch and my teeth drop inside them. My mouth is hollow like a ball inside. It's like a cave. It's hot and round and humming. My lips part. It sounds like a drop of water. I say it again.

'Momma—'

'Mmmm?'

She almost sounds like she's singing. It's one clean note sliding up.

I see her profile half from the side and back, her dark brown hair. Her skin is soft and light. Her skin is one smooth line of profile from her forehead to her slightly open mouth, her chin, her neck, white, down into her white blouse. Her eyes look up at the closet shelf. I see her eyelashes curving like backwards Cs. They're long and black, not thin like the shiny hairy threads on the edge of her wool slacks, but thick and smooth.

Everything is smooth. Everything is still and I can see everything and everything is clean. The shiny brass-coloured doorknob on the front door reflects the overhead entry hall light. I can see the jerk of the shiny gold second hand and a little window of reflection on the convex face of the mantel clock in the room with the hard-soft chairs. I can see a *Field and Stream* rolled up behind one leg of the far hard-soft chair. Everything is still and permanent. Everything is in its place and I know where everything is.

My mother is reaching back in the closet for a wool scarf for me to wear outside. Everything is quiet. It sounds so loud when I say, 'Momma—'

Except it isn't quiet inside me. It sounds like a carnival inside me. I feel all buzzy inside me like I want to run and I want to take a nap and I have to go to the bathroom. I can see everything and hear everything, my big brother outside laughing and the second hand clicking and the hangers in the closet swaying from where the coat came out and the 'psss' of the funny radiator in Stan's room upstairs and the thap of cold white balls breaking and my heart beating and my temples. I can see the rim of my glasses and the dirt on the lenses and those animals that slide over your eyeballs sometimes, and I can feel my blood pulsing and going to my fingers and head and I can hear my ears make sounds like they do against my pillow at night and I can feel how heavy my clothes are and I can see the things in the closet: boxes and coats and hats and umbrellas and two tennis racquets and the binoculars case and a vacuum cleaner and shoes and plastic shoe-covers and big plastic bags for dry cleaning and caps and scarves.

And my mother, and I say, 'Momma—'

And she says, 'Mmmm?'

She reaches for the cap on the shelf, leans down to put it on me. 'What honey?' She pats my hair and pulls the cap down over my ears. She tucks my bangs in front. I look right at her. She looks at me when she finishes and waits for me to say something. My throat stings. I can barely whisper, 'Momma— Momma—'

'What honey?' She looks at me. 'You OK, baby?'

I nod.

'You sure?'

I nod again.

She puts the back of her cool hand to my forehead to test for fever. Her hand is soft against my skin. I close my eyes. I can feel blood going all through the blue veins in her hands. She takes her hand away. It's cool where her hand was. I open my eyes. 'You're OK,' she says.

I nod. My throat still stings. I want to say something to her. I want to tell her something. I want to say, 'Momma—'

She looks at me, touches my cheek, stands up. She pulls me up by my arm and walks me to the door. Her hand is on my shoulder. I reach up to open the door with her. Cold air hits me. Everything is white. I stand there a second before I go out. I'm glad I've been bundled up tight and warm.

This is my first experience with snow.

II

It was black outside. My mother woke me up. She leaned over me and said. 'Honey, honey, it's time.' She was warm and she smelled like bacon and eggs. It was the earliest I'd ever woken up and I was thrilled. I wanted to shout but I had to be quiet because Stan was still asleep. This was the first time I got to go with my father. Even though Stan and I were only a year apart, he got to do everything. When I told Stan it wasn't fair and that we should flip on it, he said OK and I won. So Stan had to go to school and bring me my homework and I got to go out. I'd been lucky and beaten my brother and I liked it. I kept especially quiet when I went downstairs. It wasn't Stan, it was only my parents and me awake.

I sat down at the white kitchen table and ate my cereal. My father had been up for a while. He had already eaten and was packing stuff for the trip by the door. Some friends of his were coming to pick us up. I'd almost gotten dressed by myself, but my mother finished dressing me in the heavy hunting stuff. 'Stick your foot out.' She wedged my thickly socked foot into my brother's boot.

I tried to feel an Alpha-bit letter with my tongue. I was eating Alpha-bit cereal. I was good at feeling the letters in Alpha-bit cereal. They were bigger and harder and stayed solid longer than the little pasta digits in alphabet soup. I found the letter 'D'. It was an easy one. I leaned down to my mother who was lacing up the boot. I whispered, 'D, Momma. D for ducks and Daddy.'

She didn't understand me. She whispered back. 'What?'

'D. For ducks and Daddy.'

She smiled. We were whispering so we wouldn't wake my brother.

She finished lacing up the thick cords in the big olive-green boots. She asked me if I'd been to the bathroom and I said yea. Then my father said, 'They're here,' so I got up from the table. My mother put a big beige scarf around my head. My glasses steamed and I could feel my breath turning into drops where the scarf was against my nose. I wore Stan's black wool cap and his old jacket. My mother gave me the lunches to carry while my father and his friends packed the car. I stood by the car watching them and looking up at the sky. Everything was dark and clear. The sun wouldn't be up for a long time. My mother stood inside the door. She handed them their coats and flashlights and leather bags and binoculars and thermoses. They got the guns themselves.

There was no one out, just my father and his friends and me. I sat in the back and leaned my head all the way back and looked up at the stars. We went to a place that seemed like forever to get there and I fell asleep. I woke up when we were going through this little village. The car went bumpy all of the sudden on a dirt road. It was just getting light. I saw two skinny boys with black hair chasing geese around in the road. The geese were screaming. We almost ran into them and I was afraid we would hit one of them and kill it.

We stopped the car just outside this village and walked across a field. It was ploughed so the ground went up and down like a string of Ws lying beside each other. It was frozen and icy and crunched beneath our boots. We carried the hunting stuff across the field to where a man and his two dogs were waiting by a grey lake with two boats. We got in the boats and rowed out on to the lake to a group of reeds. The lake was like my parents' coffee cups with steam coming off. The sky was starting to get purple.

I was with my father. He and I were in one boat in one clump of reeds. The other boat was in another clump of reeds. I was responsible for holding on to the reeds so we wouldn't float away. They were tall and gold and beige and stiff so I had to hold them still or the ducks would know we were there. We were trying to stay secret.

My father had told me not to talk once we got on the water because you could hear everything on the water, and we could. I could hear the other boat's paddle dipping even when they were far away. I could hear my father breathing as he pulled the oars back. I could hear the water when the boat went through it like unthreading a zipper.

When both boats were settled and everything was quiet, I heard something from the shore. The man and his hunting dogs were running in the field to scare up the ducks. My father crouched on his feet holding his rifle. His face looked like he was going to jump. He didn't turn when I looked at him. He was looking at the sky. Someone screamed. The man on shore and the dogs started screaming and yipping. I looked at my father. 'Daddy—'

'Ssshhh—' my father spun his rifle around. I felt the boat tip.

I grabbed the reeds. They cracked in my hands. I closed my eyes. My father jumped. The boat tipped. There were shots in the air. My ears were popping hard, hard, only on the outside. I let go of the reeds and held on to the boat. I held tight.

'Got 'em!' my father whispered, but he sounded like he was at a football game. I opened my eyes. He was smiling. He started rowing out of the reeds. I'd got down into the bottom of the boat. He didn't notice. 'We got some birds,' he said.

We started rowing across the lake. I didn't know where we were going. I looked around. I saw the other boat. The men in the other boat waved and my father waved back. Then he held up three fingers in the black glove of his hand. He pointed to the binoculars case. I handed them to him. He stopped rowing and put the binoculars up to his eyes and looked around. He was looking for the bodies of the dead ducks. We rowed over to one and we came up to it and it was dead. It was lying on top of the water. It was floating, but it was dead. Its neck was smashed. It was a mallard drake. Stan had showed me a picture of one in a book. They had beautiful dark green heads, only this one had red-brown marks all over it.

We slid up to it. My father stopped rowing and grabbed the duck with the fish net and dropped it in the boat. Some of the water splashed my face. It was cold. I looked at the duck. It was lying in water and blood. The boat smelled when it came in. My father headed for the next one. I looked at the duck. I could see where blood was streaming into the puddle of water. It was like when we studied currents in Miss Hardison's class and she poured thick red water into regular clear water to show us about currents and streams. Then we were at the next duck. My father nodded at the fishing net. I handed it to him and he threw another duck in on top of the old one. This one was brown, a hen. Then we went some more and we came to the last duck.

My father nodded to the net. I picked it up and handed it to him but he didn't take it. He said, 'You can do it.' I didn't want to, but I thought Stan would have if he was the one with our father. My father was watching me to see if I would. I leaned out of the boat and stretched my arms. The net was heavy. I got the duck and tried to lift it but it was heavy. It jolted and I screamed, 'Daddy!'

'Ssshhh!' he said, and jumped over and grabbed my arm.

The boat rocked. My father helped me bring the duck in.

'Daddy, it's alive.'

He looked at me like I was a baby. 'No, it's just heavy. Settle down.' Then he dumped it on the two other ducks. It moved.

'Daddy—'

'Ssshhh—'

I lowered my voice and pointed. 'Daddy, it's alive.'

Then he looked at the duck and said, real slow, 'Oh, shit.'

'Daddy, can't we put it back?'

'No,' he said, 'it'll never live.' He started rowing. 'We'll have to kill it,' my father said.

He was looking over his shoulder. I turned around to see what he was looking at. The other boat was signalling to my father. He raised one hand and nodded. He said to me, 'You'll have to kill it.' Then he said, 'I have to row. Here, turn around.' He held me by my shoulders and turned me around. I put my back against the seat and faced the back of the boat. He threw the live duck down at the end of the boat. It went splat when it hit the floor. Some water splashed me. 'You have to kill it,' my father said. He started rowing.

'Daddy—'

'It won't hurt when it's dead. Kill it. Put your foot up against its neck and press.'

'Daddy—' He didn't hear me. I was facing the other way. I put my foot against the duck's head and pressed it into the corner between the bottom and back of the boat.

'Use your heel,' my father said.

The duck made gurgly noises. Its eyes were opening and closing really fast. One foot was limp and the other one was shaking really fast. Its breast feathers were dirty. I pressed my brother's boot against it. I could feel the neck under my foot. It was hard. I heard the paddle slipping on the outside of the boat. Water and blood were running down the middle of the boat from the two dead ducks. This one was alive. I pressed my foot against it. It twisted. My back hurt from where I was pressing against the seat. My fingers were mashing inside my gloves. My glasses were steaming. My foot was pressing the duck's neck. I was breaking the duck's neck. The duck was alive. It was trying not to die. I was watching it die. I was making it die. I was killing it. I was killing it with my foot.

III

We didn't go back to the Richs' 'til Halloween and then we didn't both go really because Stan chickened out so I had to go by myself. But we were going to go to be nice because we thought it would be nice if some of Tommy's old friends went to see Mrs Rich and see how Tommy was. Also we thought they'd give us lots of candy on account of Mrs Rich was really nice.

So we went to the back of Tommy's house because that's the way we always used to. But when we were about to go into the yard Stan said he didn't want to go. I thought it wouldn't be nice to just turn around and leave so I said I thought we oughtta go. But Stan said he really didn't want to. He said he'd wait for me by the back gate if I wanted to go in. I said, 'What, is my little brother a chicken?' and he said, 'No, I just don't feel like going.' 'Sure,' I said really slow to make sure he knew I thought he was being chicken. I felt a little scared myself but I sure wasn't going to let him know that and besides I really did want to be nice to Mrs Rich and Tommy. Stan said he'd wait, and for me to try to get double for him so I said I'd try.

I stepped on to the grass. My hi-tops squeaked because the grass was wet because it was dark and it had been really hot. That's what happens when it turns night after a hot day – condensation, like I learned in Miss Hardison's class. I heard the squeak of my tennies, but I turned around because I also heard Stan say something.

'What?' I whispered loudly.

'You're gonna come back aren't you?' he asked.

'Of course I am,' I said like I couldn't believe he was being so dumb.

'OK, OK. Just hurry.'

How could I hurry if he kept pestering me? 'Don't leave,' I told him, 'I'll be right back.'

'OK,' he said and then he shut up. He may have been chicken, but at least he minded me.

When I turned back around I saw the pool. Leaves and dirt were in the water. There was a chain-link fence around the pool and, outside the fence, chairs and a table. You could swim almost all the time it was so warm. That's one reason Mom said we might as well stay, because the weather was so nice. There was this light going all straight across the pool. It was the moon. I looked up and it was all white and round and I thought it would be really neat to see a witch fly by. I didn't believe in them, but I thought they were neat.

All the sudden I got a shiver. It was muggy out but my skin felt cold even under the big old raincoat I had on. I was a spy. I had all these pockets where if I wanted I could be not fair and hide my best candy, like Reeses, so that when Stan and I put our stuff together he wouldn't know I had it. He was so small he would never think of anyone doing that, like Mom and Dad had tried to do. But I wasn't going to do that because it wasn't fair, but I did think about it. I also had on this old hat that smelled like Dad and chemical mothballs. I had on sunglasses, regular not prescription, because last time I was at the eye doctor she said I didn't need them anymore. And I had on black leather gloves that Stan and I had found when we were rooting around looking for costume stuff. Stan and I were sick of all the boring ghost and witch and beatnik and hobo stuff that everybody always wore. A pirate, which Stan was, wasn't really all that great either, but we made him a really cool one with scars on his face and black shadows and tattoos all over. We spent all day making tattoos on him and some on me too even though I was a spy. He had a skull and crossbones and TNT going off and dripping daggers we'd put on with Bic pens.

I wished I could tiptoe quietly in Mrs Rich's yard but it was so squeaky and my trick-or-treat bag kept banging against my leg when I walked. It was a brown-paper grocery bag which would usually be turned into a garbage bag under the sink, but we'd stapled handles on it and painted witches and stuff. Mom laughed because she said we were going out to collect garbage because she called all the candy garbage food and said it would kill us, but she let us go anyway and actually seemed to have fun kidding us.

My bag wasn't very full but I knew I had some good stuff. A lot of gum and those peanut-buttery sort of ones the PTA sell that come in orange and black wax paper and lots of those individually cellophane-wrapped ones that you can't see what they are but they're hard and supposed to be fruit flavours or jawbreakers. I had a couple of neat little mini boxes of Hot Tamales and Good 'n Plenty and two popcorn balls and a caramel apple. I never really liked them and I considered them dumb. I mean, you figure it takes a real long time to make them and they just get all messy in your sack if they fall out of the baggie. Also it was in the newspaper about a guy who put razor blades in apples. I wouldn't have eaten one anyway though. That's on account of Stan really liked sticky stuff so he'd always trade me. I'd usually get a chocolate bar or something good for each. If it was a really big one, he'd give me a Reeses and that was really worth it.

So I went up to the back porch of Mrs Rich's and was gonna knock on the door. It was a sliding glass door and the curtains were open so Mrs Rich saw me before I knocked and she slid the door open and said, 'Well, who's this?' but she was faking. She knew who I was. 'Trick or treat,' I said and she turned back to Bruce, her boyfriend. Bruce was sitting in the room and she said, 'Well, honey, what'll it be?' and he said, 'Ask her what the trick is.' So Mrs Rich said, 'What's the trick?' and I said well I didn't really know, but she didn't let me finish. She laughed and put her arm around me and brought me inside. Bruce got up and said, 'Well, if you don't have a trick, we'll just have to treat, huh?' He was a very nice guy, but not very cool. I said yea and Mrs Rich put a whole gob of candy in my bag. All chocolate. Then she said, 'You're not trick or treating by yourself are you?' Stan and I used to go with Tommy and John. I said no, that I was with Stan but he was over down the street waiting for a friend and I was gonna meet them in a few minutes. I made that up – well, lied actually – but I figured it was OK even if it wasn't true because I didn't think it would be nice for me to say that Stan thought it was too creepy.

Mrs Rich said, 'Stan's all by himself?' like she was scared and I said that his friend was right on his way and I was going to meet them. Then Bruce jumped in and said really jolly, 'Well, why don't we give you extra for them?' I said that was OK, that they didn't have to. But Bruce was putting all this candy in my sack and he winked at me and said in a fake whisper, 'They'll never know if you just keep it all to yourself.' I think he wanted me to laugh so I did.

16

Then Mrs Rich said why didn't I sit down for just a minute and have some punch and cookies and I said well sure because I didn't want to seem like I didn't like them.

We went further into the den where there was this card table with a huge bowl of punch on it. Hawaiian punch or something and a ton of cookies. Sugar cookies mostly, home-made ones with black and orange frosting, shaped like moons and pumpkins and witches and skulls. I got a pumpkin and a witch and an orange napkin with one of those horns with squashes and corn and stuff painted on it and a cup of punch. It looked like they were about to have a party. Mrs Rich poured herself and Bruce some punch too. He said, 'Thanks, honey.' Mrs Rich said, 'We just thought we'd have some punch and cookies here in case any of you kids wanted to come inside and rest for a while instead of having to move from house to house without stopping or having to go all the way home to sit down.' Then she said very politely, 'Why don't you sit down?' So I did and that's when I saw Tommy.

He was in the next room. He didn't really look like Tommy. He looked like he was asleep. His face was dark and skinny. He was on this board sort of thing that was really his bed. It wasn't flat but it wasn't up and down either. It was sort of an angle. I thought he would fall off but then I saw that he was strapped on to it by his feet and arms in the middle right over his number because he was wearing his football shirt.

Mrs Rich saw me looking and then she asked me if I wanted some more punch and I said thanks but I had plenty. Then she said that she had thought it would be nice if us kids wanted to have a break from trick or treating that we could come and have some punch. She'd just said sort of the same thing. I think Bruce remembered that because he looked at her. Then Mrs Rich said, 'And besides, we just haven't seen very much of you kids in such a long time. I just thought it would be nice to see you.'

At first nobody was allowed to come until they got the chain-link fence up and then everybody was used to not coming so nobody came anymore and besides Tommy was really sick and John stopped hanging around.

I'd never seen Tommy since then. I saw him sort of when they got him out, but there were some people around so I couldn't really see. I just kept looking and looking at him lying there on that board. He didn't look like he was asleep and I knew I could never sleep lying crooked like that. I didn't think he'd get better. I wasn't supposed to tell, but I heard someone say that he really shouldn't be alive anymore anyway. It was that day when they found out he sort of was. Stan and I were just coming over. We had on our swimming suits and flip-flops and Stan said I was a chicken on account of I was afraid to take them off just because Mom said not to but I told him she didn't make me wear them. I just wore them because I felt like it. Then Stan said, race you, so we had to take them off and we ran, which was stupid because I always won. But Stan kept saying that one of these days he'd get big enough to outrun me. I'd stopped trying to explain that even though he would get bigger, I'd still keep getting bigger too and I'd always be able to go faster than him. But that day I dropped my towel so I had to stop and pick it up so he was there before me, so in a way he did win, but it hadn't been fair. When I got there I was all sweaty and panting and Stan was standing outside their yard and I said, 'What are you—' but I didn't finish. He was looking in the Richs' yard. Mr Schneider, he's their next door neighbour, he was in the pool but he had his clothes on. Mrs Rich was standing by the pool in her bathrobe folding her hands over and over. Mr Schneider was swimming with Tommy. He came out of the water with Tommy and stretched him out on the side of the pool and started hitting him on the back. Mrs Rich wasn't screaming but she was making a high-low noise. Bruce came out behind her. He only had on his jeans and he tried to put his arm around her but she didn't move so he went away. Mr Schneider leaned over Tommy and gave him artificial respir-ators. We had to do that in Juniors on each other, all except the actual kissing part because you shouldn't do that unless it's a real emergency, but this was one because Mr Schneider was really doing it.

Some hospital guys ran in the yard. They acted like Stan and I weren't there. They bumped into us so Stan and I got out of their way. We went into the yard. There were three hospital guys. Mr Schneider helped two of them with Tommy and one of them talked to Mrs Rich and Bruce. Mrs Rich was acting crazy. Bruce had his hands way down in the pockets of his jeans. His arms were perfectly straight but shaky. Then Mrs Rich was crawling around all over Tommy. She kept crying and making that noise and she didn't even care that she got all wet from hugging Tommy.

Then John came out of the sliding doors. He was still in his bathing suit but he was all dry and one of the hospital guys came over to him. Mr Schneider and the other guy took Tommy out to the street. Stan went out behind them and looked. The other guy talked to John and John kept folding his arms over his stomach and pressing. Then Mrs Rich and the hospital guys went out to their ambulance. They walked right past me like they didn't even see me. Mr Schneider said 'C'mon' to John and Bruce but they didn't do anything. Mr Schneider went over and took Bruce's hands out of his pockets and hugged him a couple times really hard and Bruce said something. Then Mr Schneider squeezed Bruce's shoulders and said 'C'mon.' Then he put his arm around John and sort of pulled him along and they took Mr Schneider's car.

Mrs Rich and one of the hospital guys got in the back of the hospital van. The other guy stopped by the front door before he got in and I heard him say to the other guy that was driving, 'Don't bother rushing Mike, he's good as gone.' Then they got in and slammed the door. The ambulance started screaming and the red light was going on and off and around and screaming.

They left so fast they left the house open. After everyone was gone Stan said, 'You hear that?' about what they said about Tommy. I nodded and Stan said, 'Let's get outta here,' but I said we couldn't just leave. Stan just stood there holding his towel really tight with both hands. I could tell how tight he was holding it by the blue veins sticking out on his hands. But we couldn't just leave, I said again, we had to do something. Then I saw the sliding glass door open so I said we had to close the door at least.

So I went back in the yard and I felt really creepy. I wasn't anywhere near the pool but I felt like it could just grab me. I didn't want to run because I was afraid I'd fall. I kept thinking something was gonna jump. I went up and slid the door closed and I saw myself reflected in the glass door, and the pool behind me. The water was blue and wavy from where Mr Schneider had been swimming and there was a long mess of puddles at the side where they'd pulled Tommy out. I didn't want to go back by the pool but I wanted to get out of the Richs' yard. I ran across the yard as fast as I could by the pool. 'Run!' I yelled at Stan. He dropped his towel and we ran all the way home barefooted. Stan was so scared he kept up with me, but also I slowed a little so he could. I slowed down for him because I knew I should, but I wished I didn't have to because I really wanted to get away from there fast.

Stan stubbed his toe and was all bloody when we got home. Mom asked us what happened and I told her. 'Oh my god,' she said. She picked Stan up and put him on the counter by the sink and washed his foot right there and told me to go get band-aids and a clean towel from the bathroom. When I came back she finished fixing Stan. He wasn't whining at all. She did it real quick. 'Here, why don't you guys have a snack.' She grabbed some Twinkies out of the cupboard and threw them on the counter and poured us some Kool-Aid real fast and didn't wipe it up when it spilled. 'Now why don't you guys go watch some TV,' she said. She shoo-ed us into the living room and told us if we wanted more I could get us some without asking her permission. While Stan and I tried to watch Cartoon Carnival I heard Mom talking to somebody on the phone. Mom and Mrs Rich were really good friends, especially since they were divorced.

So when Mrs Rich said to me on Halloween, 'Well, aren't you going to meet Stan?' and I said yea, and Mrs Rich said, 'Well, don't walk by yourself. John will walk you down there,' I had to say OK. I couldn't say that I had been faking because Stan was just waiting for me right outside their yard because he didn't want to come in because he thought it was too creepy.

I wanted to get going because I'd taken longer than I thought and Stan was still waiting. At least I hoped he hadn't left. Then Mrs Rich said, 'You just need to be careful you know. You never can tell what could happen and John won't mind. John!' Mrs Rich and Bruce and I stood around and didn't say anything while we waited for John. I looked when he came downstairs and I saw Tommy again. He looked just the same. Lying on the board with his skinny dark face.

John said hi and I said hi. Mrs Rich said, 'You'll just take a little walk down the street, won't you? This mysterious spy here—' Bruce winked at me when she said that – 'is going to meet her little brother Stan and his friend there.' John said OK, but he didn't sound like he really wanted to.

John used to go trick or treating with us even though he used to make jokes about Tommy being such a pest who'd want to be around him; but John didn't go trick or treating any more. Last year John didn't dress up but he went with us and stood down at the end of the yards and waited for us and we gave him some of our candy. Going with John was better than going with somebody's Mom or Dad or by yourself because if you went by yourself you weren't allowed to go very far or stay out very late, but you couldn't get away with anything with somebody's parents. Besides, John was really nice, especially for an old guy. He was really funny too. He cracked all sorts of jokes. I hadn't seen him much since this summer though. He was in Junior High and it was after Tommy and all. So nobody really hung around there anymore.

Mrs Rich gave me another cookie. I thanked her for the treats and punch and cookies and she put her arm around me and said, 'Now you and Stan come play here any time you want. Bruce and I are glad to see you any time.' I said thanks again and she kept saying, 'You can bring some of your school friends too. We've just gotten a new colour TV so you can come watch colour TV if you want.' She nodded into the den where the TV was. It was really huge. I thought it would be great to see Batman in colour or Cartoon Carnival on a huge TV like that.

Then John and I left. We went out the sliding glass door. He closed it behind us and we went across the porch. We stepped off the porch and were out of the light of the house. We started squeaking across the yard not saying anything. I couldn't think of anything to say even though I hadn't seen John for ages. Stan was at the edge of the yard. He was facing the other way. He turned around when he heard us and said,· 'What took you so— oh, hi John.' He didn't expect to see John. John said hi to Stan, how you doing. Stan said he was OK and asked John how he was and he said he was OK. Stan asked John if he was going trick or treating and John said nah. Stan said that he and I could give him some of our stuff. But John said that was OK, they had tons of stuff at home because Bruce had bought tons and his Mom had bought tons too. They did have tons of stuff, but I figured John might like to go trick or treating anyway.

'Whadya get?' he asked Stan. Stan opened his bag and started digging around. 'Oh you know, gum, peanut butter logs, popcorn balls, Mr Goodbars, a caramel apple, some Reeses, PTA candy . . .' John said, 'That's a real haul,' and then he asked me if me or Stan had any Sweetarts. John really liked Sweetarts. Stan and I looked into our bags and felt around but we couldn't see anything.

'I don't know, I can't see,' Stan said, and I said, 'Me neither.'

John said he'd really like some Sweetarts and would it be OK if he paid us back some chocolate from his house. We said he didn't have to pay us back, but we'd have to dump our bags out to see and we couldn't do that in the street and I knew Stan wouldn't want to go inside with Tommy. John said we could use the table by the pool. There was still some moonlight because there weren't trees by the pool. Stan said, 'Is that OK?' He really had the creeps. Mom had said she'd let me take Stan out alone, without someone older like John or her if I was really careful and watched him and didn't let him get scared. But I thought it was OK since the fence was up. 'Sure it's· OK,' I said. But John said to Stan, 'We don't have to go if you don't want to Stan.' John was really careful to not make a little guy like Stan do something he wasn't up to. But Stan didn't want to hurt John's feelings. Stan said, 'No, no, no. It's not creepy, I just wanted to make sure it was OK.' John waited for a second like he thought Stan was going to say something else. Stan looked down at the ground then bent down to tie his shoe which didn't need tying.

Nobody said anything so I turned around and walked back into the yard like it was no big deal. Then Stan and John came in too. We went near the pool but on the outside of the fence. You could just see little squares of the pool through the fence. John went over to the table and pulled out a chair. The chairs were really close to the table like they hadn't been sat in. I pulled a chair out too. It was heavy and it scraped along on the concrete. We pulled out another one for Stan. We all sat down. Stan and I dumped our bags out on the glass-top table. I could see Stan's and John's and my sneakers through the glass. John's were touching the ground. They were his Chuck Taylor Converse All-Star basketball hi-tops. He was on the team. Stan and I had on K-Mart hi-tops, but if you hid the ankles with the bottoms of your jeans, you almost couldn't tell they weren't Chucks. My feet were against the pole under the table and Stan's were just hanging in the air.

We dumped our candy on the table. We dumped both our bags together because it didn't matter who got what because Stan and I were partners and we went halfies on everything. I pushed up the sleeves of my huge raincoat and took off my gloves and started looking for Sweetarts. There was a lot of candy. When John saw Stan's and my tattoos, he said, 'Pretty cool.' I shrugged, then Stan did too, like it was no big deal. 'You guys do that yourselves?' John asked. I nodded and so did Stan.

We rooted around in the stuff for a while and Stan said, 'Too bad you're not out this year, John. We got lots of great stuff.' 'Yea,' said John. Stan picked up a jawbreaker and glanced at me. I nodded and Stan gave it to John. It was the closest thing, though of course it really wasn't close at all, to a Sweetart. John said thanks, but then he said, really suddenly, 'Hey, what about your friend, Stan?' and Stan said, 'Huh?' Then I had to tell John that it was just a lie I made up because I didn't want to say that Stan was outside but didn't want to come in. 'Honest, John,' I said, 'It's not that it's creepy. It's just that Stan didn't feel like it—'

'It is too creepy,' John said. 'It's totally creepy.'

Nobody said anything. Then John picked up the jawbreaker, I heard the paper crackle in his hands, and threw it over the fence into the pool. It went – plop – and made circles that got bigger until they got to the edge. 'That's where they got him out,' John said. He'd thrown the jawbreaker in the deep end. 'And that—' he turned around and threw a Banana Bike up at his window on the second floor. It sounded like tap. '—is where I was. And that—' He threw one of those cellophane-wrapped hard candies over the fence on the pavement by the pool. It made a crack, '—is where I was supposed to be. I was supposed to be watching Tommy.' John was a really good swimmer. He was going to be a Junior Life Saver. 'I was supposed to be watching him,' John said. He said it really slow like he was telling someone else. I looked over at Stan. The black marks on his pirate face made him look really skinny and shadowy. He was looking at John. 'I was watching my brother only I went up to my room to put some more glue on my model airplane but it was broken so I took a long time and I forgot him.' He didn't say anything for a few seconds. 'I came down when Mom started screaming.'

No one said anything so I said, 'I think Tommy is going to get better, John.' Then John said again, like he didn't hear, 'I didn't mean to leave him.'

'I really do think Tommy will get better soon, John. I really do,' I said again. Then it was quiet.

Then John said, not to me or Stan, or anyone really, not looking at us, really quiet, that he hoped Tommy would die. We were all really quiet. Then John said that Tommy just lied there all day and didn't do anything and his Mom never stopped going on about Tommy getting better and that every time people came over, even though hardly anybody ever came over, they saw Tommy and thought it was really creepy and wouldn't look at him anymore, him being John. But Stan and I were looking at John. Stan was staring at him.

I could hear the quiet licking of the water against the pool. It was those circles of ripples where John had thrown that piece of candy. I looked through the checks of the chain-link fence down at the deep end of the pool. The checks made it look like there were millions of little square pools all stacked against each other, millions. I imagined that jawbreaker sunk down in the deep end inside the wet cellophane wrapper. I thought how if it stayed there it would get smaller, layer by layer, wearing down from purple to blue to red to black to white until there was nothing left inside the empty wrapper.

I looked over at John. John was looking at Stan. Stan was picking through the candy on the table, picking through it again as if we'd missed something the first time that he could give to John but there wasn't.

2

The Lost Boy

My baby brother Stan was playing in the market place. He wanted me to play with him but I didn't want to. He was at that age when babies aren't content to entertain themselves, but don't know how to play fairly with someone else, and I wasn't about to compromise on my idea of fair. I couldn't exactly walk off and leave him though; I was supposed to be watching him.

Stan had found the biggest, muddiest puddle by the water pump in the middle of the square. He splashed along making a complete mess of himself but I didn't stop him. He was only in his diaper and he'd probably have to have it changed about every two minutes because he was such a shit-bucket. So when he did need changing, I'd just dunk him all the way under the water pump. The sun was out, he'd dry quickly. I could see some of the mud dry on him. The streaks lightened from dark, blood-coloured brown to cocoa, then flaked off.

Stan stuck his hands in the puddle and slapped mud all over his fat, naked tummy. He grunted syllables like 'Nnnng' and 'Mmmmb'. The suddenly he squeaked, 'Dwaaaa!', looked up at me and demanded, in the special private language of a prima donna, 'Bwoong?' When I rolled my eyes and dismissed him with an unenthusiastic, 'Great, Stan,' he fussed. He thwapped his hands in the mud and insisted, 'Ming! Ming! Ming!' I tried to look impressed enough to shut him up, while retaining the haughty dignity of an older sister. I was in my I-don't-care-about-you phase. My most common gesture was to cross my arms over my no longer entirely flat chest, roll my eyes, and give an extremely subtle shrug of my shoulders. This indicated that, while I was too mature to be taken in by his infantile antics, I didn't care enough to bother arguing about something so trivial. Still, I had to admit that Stan was a cute little kid, even if he got things I never had when I was his age, which he didn't deserve, even if everybody made too much of a fuss over him, and gave less attention to me, even if I had to watch him, i.e. pay just enough attention so I wouldn't get in trouble or damage my reputation as a hard-working, reliable older kid. When I wasn't watching him, I was gazing dreamily at the flag that flew over the Great Hall, and wishing I was somewhere else.

Across the square, over by the butcher's stall, some guys were playing tag. A bunch of girls were playing jacks on the flat smooth

27

flagstones behind us. In front of the Great Hall a skinny, droopy-shouldered kid held the reins of a horse which obviously belonged to some tyrannical adult who didn't care if they forced some poor squirt to stand around imitating a hitching post. Three or four really stupid girls sat on some logs that were stacked near the outer gate and cooed over a bundle of hay they'd wrapped up in a patriotic red and blue scarf to look like a baby. Two brats with skinned knees and cut-offs were trying to sell the eggs they'd just stolen from the chicken coop up the road. As if any kid in her right mind would waste decent allowance money on eggs. I was sitting on this orange crate I'd dragged over just waiting for one of those eggs to start flying and those stupid girls to start squealing.

Oblivious to all of this, Stan was making very runny mud pies. Actually, something more like mud shakes. He wiggled his fingers then patted his hands together, then patted his hands against the surface of the mud puddle. He scooped up a couple of fistfuls of mud and squished it between his fingers and screeched. He seemed perfectly – and it bugged me to see it – happy.

Then suddenly he dropped his hands and crawled over to me. He plopped back on his dirty butt and stretched his muddy hands up like he wanted me to hold him. I looked down at the mess he was, rolled my eyes and sighed my I-don't-care sigh. But he shook his hands like he really meant it. 'Awww, c'mon, Stan,' I whined. A horse across the courtyard began to neigh, then do a high, weird whinny. When I looked up, it was stamping its feet and swinging its head back and forth in the bit. Then a dog lowered its leg mid-pee, stuck his nose up in the air and howled a long, thin howl. Stan made a gurgly noise. I didn't look at him, but lifted my half-cupped palm and pretended to examine a violet smudge on the back of my hand.

'Don't leave,' I heard a voice whisper, sort of like when you hear a voice in your head. Then I heard it again. *'Don't leave me.'* Only this time the voice seemed to be coming from outside, from below me. I looked down at Stan. His soft pink baby lips were pressed white and flat, like he was telling a secret. He opened his toothless mouth: *'Don't leave,'* he shook his arms insistently. I picked him up.

'Stan?' Even though I whispered, his hair was so fine it blew. 'Stan, did you just talk—'

He shushed me, scraping his tiny baby fingernails, as small as dots, against my forearm. I looked down at his hands and saw the faint blue-purple lines that surfaced on his skin when he was afraid or excited. I held him close, my arms across his back and bottom. The hair on his head was soft and pale. His skin was moist and clammy and so thin I could feel his pulse from every part of him that touched my body. His chubby legs dangled. I felt his toes curl by my stomach and his fingers clutch my forearms. His body was warm.

'Stan?' I whispered.

Across the square, the chickens in cages started squawking the way they do in the morning when the butcher comes. The girls playing baby-doll looked up. I heard a wet clapping noise and looked down to see Stan's mouth closed tight; his gums were chattering. He wrenched his arms free from mine, squeezed his eyes closed and stuck his fingers in his ears.

'Stan?'

Then I heard the siren. It was a wail, a long high cry, the terrible three minute warning. None of us had heard it before, but we all knew what it was.

Everybody moved. The girls dropped their doll and ran. The kid with the reins jumped on to the horse's back and bolted. Cows and oxen broke loose from carts. Birds screeched. I leapt, but Stan dug his baby fingers into me: *'Don't leave me.'*

I felt the sudden weight of Stan, his tubby legs, his pudgy tummy, his baggy diaper. He was too small to run, but too big for me to carry.

Around us toddlers grabbed bigger kids who struggled to be let go. Wimpy guys in Little Lord Fauntleroy haircuts tore across the cobblestones in their pointy, slipper-like shoes. Girls in capes and high-pointed hats rushed by us. Boys just beginning to get moustache fuzz dropped their basketballs and baseball bats and ran on their gangly legs. The two brats with the eggs dropped them, knocked a fat boy off his bike and jumped, one on the seat, the other on the handle bars, and pedalled away like mad. Nobody, not the tobacco-chewing toughs at the cigarette stand, or the ragged hicks in overalls, or the beardless soldiers in their bright red and blue striped shirts, knew where they were going but everybody ran.

Everybody, that is, except my brother.

I wanted to run, but Stan, with one squeeze of his tiny hand, and one sad look of his eyes, made me not leave. I sat back down on the orange crate and held him firmly in my lap. Calm as a buddha, my brother told me, 'Watch them'.

Then, above the panic in the market place, we saw two figures climb up the roof of the Great Hall. Their silhouettes were dark against the flaming orange sky. They cast huge shadows over us like fast moving clouds. Smoke rose up through the roof of the Great Hall. Some of the escaping kids glanced up to see what darkened and illuminated them, but only my brother, and me, because he made me, watched.

We watched the two big bodies press against each other. Their tight hands grabbed and struggled with the pole of the flag between them. Stan didn't fidget in my lap, but stared up at them, rapt. I squinted to try to see them clearly, but I couldn't.

'One of us may get out . . .' Stan said softly.

He shook my sweaty hands off him, and slipped to the ground. My suddenly empty arms began to shake. 'Stan—' I started to protest.

My brother held his hand up to silence me. 'I'll try to stop them,' he said.

He took my too-big hands in his and whispered slowly, as if he could make me understand. 'Watch me. Do not forget. Don't be like them.'

My brother looked so serious, and so intent, as if he knew something enough, believed something enough, for both of us. So when he said, 'Don't tell the lie,' I blurted, 'I won't.' But I didn't know what my brother was saying. I didn't know what I promised him.

My brother pressed my hands together in his. I felt the soft dampness of his palms against my wrinkly knuckles. He couldn't cover my hands with his. He squeezed my hands tightly once, then released them.

'Where are you going?'

'Back,' my brother said.

I saw the thin, light-aqua-blue lines of the veins in his scalp, and the gentle dip near the centre of his skull. I saw his tiny naked back, the dimples at the base of his spine above his diaper line. I saw, and I remembered when I'd touched, when I had slept beside him, the perfect, tender, milk-coloured creases of the insides of his elbows. I thought of the scent of his sweet sleeping breath.

I saw his mouth open but I couldn't hear what he said beneath the sounds of civil war. My brother pulled me to him so close I felt the warmth of his breath and skin. He said, 'Don't be like them. Don't leave.'

And then, my brother left.

My brother walked, on his unsteady baby legs, into the square. Horses stampeded and dogs snapped their teeth, but my brother didn't swerve from his path. He was walking towards the Great Hall where they fought. Through the crush of legs and wheels and feet between us, I saw bits of my brother's rose-coloured skin. I saw him fling his blue-splotched baby hand up high, and then his body fell.

I ran. I grabbed my orange crate and ran to the far corner of the square. I huddled down behind the crate, knees to chest, head tucked low, eyes closed. I didn't want to watch, but I couldn't keep out the sounds. I heard the two of them shout terrible things to one another. I heard gunshots and exploding bombs. I heard the plants and coffee cups and china and glass they threw at each other break. I heard the slow agonized creak of falling walls, the crush of people's bodies pinned beneath.

When I heard the crack, as close as if it had been next to me, as if it was a bone that broke inside of me, my eyes popped open. I peeked out between the slats of the crate and saw careening carts and cars. I didn't see my brother.

I looked up at the roof where the two figures fought. They'd cracked the pole. I heard the whup of a billow of cloth. I squinted into the smoky sky and saw each of them grab, with their black-gloved hands, a corner of the flag and pull. They ripped the flag along the seam that bound the red stripe to the blue. When the cloth was split, each of them swished their half in a fluttery arc, then jumped off opposite sides of the roof. When their feet hit the ground, the Great Hall exploded behind them.

'Don't leave!' I shouted, but I was too late.

Each of them gathered terrified kids behind their strips of cloth and ran away from each other. I watched until they ran out of sight.

I looked through the cracks of the crate at the place where Stan had fallen, but nothing moved. I listened to the quiet weeping sounds of sizzling coals and crumbling ash. Smoke and dust rose from the deserted city. The air was thick. I felt like I was breathing blood. When I blinked, it felt like water.

After a while, the sky started getting thinner. Gradually, it turned silvery grey, then milky-white, as if the sky was gauze with a light behind it. After a longer while, I saw some spots moving in the gauze. The shapes got bigger, moved closer: children. Ragged, they tiptoed back. Furtively looking right and left, they picked through piles of broken things. When they spoke, they whispered. Some of them piled the things they recovered into little red wagons. I saw a boy sorting through a heap where the Great Hall had been. He suddenly broke into sobs, and the girl with him shook him by his shoulders then put her hand on his mouth to shush him. A few of them dragged small bodies out from the fallen beams and put them in a cart. The stiff, charred arms and legs poked out like sticks.

The children didn't stay long. They shuffled back into the pale mauve horizon. I didn't see where they went. After a long time, two gangs of kids came back; from one side in reddish uniforms, and from the other in blue. They wore ski-masks and kicked through the debris. They slapped each other around and shouted. Fistfights broke out between them as they divvied up the wreckage. What there were two of were divided one to each: his and her crowns and thrones and monogrammed towels, one of the country homes to each, to each one of the gardens. What there was only one of was divided by equivalent values: one got the army, the other the schools; one got the trains, the other got the stables; one got the tape deck, the other the VCR. The gangs accused each other of stealing or destroying what had been lost. What couldn't be agreed upon was axed, then trampled underfoot, then left.

When they dragged their shovels over the spot where I had last seen Stan, I held my breath. But they didn't pull anything up. After the rubble was divided, they went back to their separate sides.

It was quiet for a long time before I dragged my crate back out to the centre of the former market place where I had lost my brother. Directly across from where the Great Hall had been, I sat on my crate, hugged my knees up to my chest and bowed my head. I wanted, though my brother had told me not to, to forget.

When I opened my eyes, I was still sitting on top of my crate, but my crate was sitting on top of a wall. It was a brick wall, about three feet wide and stretching in front and behind me as far as I could see. In the dusky light on either side of the wall I saw two faint outlines of rows of tents, two constellations of campfires, and two thin flags.

I stood up, put my half-opened hand to my mouth and shouted as loudly as I could, 'Staaa-aaaan!' I heard the crackle of campfires, the whup of flags, but no sound of my brother. I took a breath and shouted again, 'Staaaaan-leeeeeey!' It was as quiet as a humid summer night.

Then I heard the shuffle of running feet. Two pairs. And the swishing of cloth and huffing breath.

'Shut-up!'

'Shut-up up there!'

I looked down to one side, then the other, but couldn't see anything clearly.

'Get off the wall!' The voice was from my left.

'Stop screeching and get off the goddamned wall!' Another voice from my right.

'I'm looking for my—' I started.

The one on the left interrupted. 'Get the hell off the goddamned wall or else!'

'But he's only a baby,' I tried to explain.

'Now!' the voice on my right bellowed. 'Get the fuck off the goddamned wall right now!'

'Somebody must have seen him,' I pleaded.

'No!'

'No!'

'No one is permitted on that goddamned wall. Now get the hell off right now!'

I sat down on my orange crate so I could look more closely at them. To my left, I could just begin to see his shiny, oily face. I tried to find his eyes to talk to him. I couldn't raise my voice much above a whisper. 'I have to find this boy—'

'Well, don't bother looking over here. *She*'s responsible for this mess—' He pointed over to the other side of the wall with his black leather glove. I turned and saw the thick dark frame of her glasses.

Meekly, I tried to explain to her, 'I was supposed to be watching my brother. Have you seen—'

'Absolutely not!' she shrieked. '*That* bastard,' she pointed back to the other side of the wall, 'is responsible for this horror—' Her black glove shook in anger.

I looked back at him.

He snorted. 'If that uppity cunt-head hadn't—' He stuck his anger-twisted face up at me. 'If she says he's here, she's lying. You can go tell her she's lying. In fact, you can tell her she can go fuck herself.'

I turned back to her. 'He says you're lying about the baby. He says—' but I couldn't bring myself to say all he'd said. I lowered my voice and tried to ask her as politely as I could, 'Are you sure you haven't seen—'

She grabbed the edge of the wall near my feet and sneered. 'You tell that bastard to go get fucked himself.'

I looked back at him. 'Um . . . she says to go get . . .' I gulped.

He kicked the wall and shook his fist up at me. 'Well you tell her to go fuck herself with an ice-pick!'

I didn't have to turn back to her. She'd grabbed my ankle and was squeezing me hard through my hi-top. Her face was trembling with rage. 'You tell that bastard—'

When she paused, I pleaded, 'What happened to—'

She snapped on, ignoring my question. 'You tell that bastard he can go stick his dick up every fucking ass in the Black Hole of Calcutta, but he's never gonna lay a filthy hand on—'

He grabbed my other ankle. 'You tell her—!'

Each of them was standing with their noses about two inches from the wall, squeezing one of my ankles. I turned my head back and forth between them. I knew they could hear and understand what each other said, because they had their retorts ready as soon as I turned to them. But they didn't speak to each other directly. And they wouldn't answer when I asked about you, Stan.

'Goddammit,' he muttered. He grabbed me by my knees and yanked me off the wall. My basketball sneakers plopped in the mud beside him. He smelled like food. He grabbed my shoulder with one hand and shook his other index finger at me. 'You get over there and tell Her Goddamned Honour that I don't have any goddamned thing of hers, and even if I did I wouldn't give it to her. You tell her—' Then he paused. 'Well, come back here and tell me what Her Tight-Assedness has to say.'

He snatched me up by my armpits and hoisted me back on to the wall. I was shivering. I could barely speak. I knelt on my hands and knees and whispered down to her. 'He says he's not—'

'What?!' She stamped. Then she pulled me off the wall. I fell at her feet. She was wearing sensible shoes. She yanked me up by my elbow. 'What did that bastard say?'

I caught my breath and repeated his message.

'Well, you can tell His Prickiness this—'

She pushed me back on top of the wall. His hands were waiting to snatch me. He made me tell the message she sent.

Thus I became their message girl.

They say that only I can speak to both of them, that only I translate their recently foreign tongues. But frankly, their languages aren't that different. All languages of romance have the same roots after all. But he won't read and she won't call and he won't listen and she won't look, so they send me.

Most of the messages they send aren't clear. They toss off words like 'Never', 'Always', 'Irreconcileable', and 'Principle' and 'Not Legitimate' like they were baby talk. I am to neither comment on, nor draw conclusions from, nor ask about, the words that I deliver. They aren't, after all, talking to me, merely through me. They each remind me, frequently, that if I don't want to run their errands, they can get rid of me. I do not ask with whom they would replace me.

They don't let me ask about you, Stan.

They each forbid their cowering citizens to cross the wall. They threaten a punishment so severe, though unspecified, that no one even dares go near the border.

Each pretends the skinny half flags flying over their two separate homes of government aren't ludicrously thin. Each pretends the part of land they have suffices – his counties and counties of overgrown woods, her miles of rusting lumberyards and mills. They each pretend that nothing is between them.

They each rewrite their histories. They try to make their followers forget.

But I have documents, a birth certificate that names a state that they claim never was.

And despite their claims to isolationism, they both grant me a special passport that takes me back and forth.

Why do they send me? I know their labour forces are only kept afloat in wartime, but I think it's more than that. I think they send me because they don't really want to be completely independent. I think that part of each of them looks back, regrets the loss.

And why do I consent?

Because, dear Stan, I know you're alive. You're hiding somewhere. You're waiting for me to find you and bring you back.

'You tell the old bitch this—' He sucks air in the hole of his mouth like a balloon blowing itself up. His oily face swells. His lips are pinched white. His cheeks and ears turn red. His fat fists tremble by his head. Then his mouth flies open and he yells, 'Go to hell, you goddamned cold-hearted bitch! Fuck you and your cunt-head demand for border realignment! Screw your starving peasants! Eat shit if you expect me to abide by some candy-ass treaty! Go fuck your own damned frigid heart out!'

He gulps a couple deep breaths then blows them out of his saggy cheeks. 'Did you get all that?'

'Yes, Your Highness.'

'OK.' He wipes his brow with a maroon silk hankie. 'Repeat it back to me.'

I start quietly, 'I'm bringing you—'

'Don't mumble fergodsake!'

I snap my head up and enunciate clearly. 'I am bringing you a message from His Highness.' I take a deep breath, just like him, then open my mouth as wide as I can and scream, 'Go to hell you goddamned cold-hearted bitch! Fuck you! . . . ' And so on.

When he's heard me recite it back the way he wants, he jerks his black-gloved thumb to dismiss me. I scurry from the Palace, barely nodding to the grey-headed old doorman who used to bob me on his knees, the smiling, toothless maid who used to coddle me. I run to the bottom of the long slim avenue of poplars and hop on the bus to the border. At the border, I flash my special passport at the two old toothless guards. They wave me through with a sympathetic shake of their old white heads or a hopeful thumbs-up signal. I read the newspaper while I take the bus to the Capitol. I get off at New Square. I hurry across the wide flagstone plaza to the Central Office. I run up the wide grey steps, flashing a wave to the interns I grew up with, the dottering old elevator man who used to tweek my ears. I mutter a quick 'hi', but can't stop to chat to the stoop-shouldered geezer who ushers me into her chamber.

She's sitting behind the huge oak desk that used to sit below a window in the Great Hall. A strand of limp grey hair falls over her dowdy, horn-rimmed People's Health glasses. She's chewing a pencil eraser as she stares intently at a sheaf of dog-eared yellow papers. She looks up at me when I'm right in front of her desk. Grey bags are under her eyes. She takes the pencil from between her teeth and sighs, 'What's the old jackass ranting about now?'

I clear my throat and recite quietly, as I do every time. 'I am bringing you a message from His Highness.'

She shakes her head and rubs her black-gloved fingertips against her temples. 'OK,' she sighs.

I straighten my shoulders, clear my throat and swallow. I hear her shift away from me in her chair. She squints as if she could keep the volume down. I yell at her as loud as I can, 'Go to hell you goddamned cold-hearted bitch! Fuck you! . . .' And so on.

After I finish, she sits in silence a few seconds, I shift back and forth from one squeaky hi-top to the other. She presses the index fingers of both hands to her temples and closes her eyes. After a few seconds, she abruptly opens her eyes. 'Take a letter.' She straightens the lapel of her plain brown suit, sniffs through her thin sharp nose and rattles out perfect paragraphs so rapidly I almost can't keep up with her: 'Capital s sir colon capital w we are in receipt of your latest communication period capital w we shall respond to your request regarding our travel arrangements to hell with a three point refutation period capital t to wit colon one close paren. . . .' And so on.

I scribble down what she says then read it back to her. She coaches me how to read it out loud. She tells me how to sound severe, to drop the ends of my sentences like knives. She shows me how to hold my head as if my chin were the blade of a guillotine. She checks my spelling and penmanship and margins. She doesn't permit smudges on her correspondence. She checks my hands for blue and purple marks and makes me wash, humiliated, if I slip.

She dismisses me with a brisk clap of her gloves. The stoop-shouldered geezer opens the door for me. I hurry back across the flagstone plaza of New Square. I catch the bus to the border. At the border I flash my passport at the smiling, geriatric guards. Sometimes one of them tosses me a wax-paper-wrapped sandwich or a Reeses Peanut Butter Cup. Sometimes I pop one in my mouth, dear Stan, and tell myself to save the other one for you.

Though I didn't realize it at the time, I'd been in training since my infancy. In fact, I owe my infancy to them.

When they first started out, everybody was amused by them. Everybody thought they were a spirited, lively pair who simply refused to sacrifice the vigorous rowdiness of youth to the lacklustre domesticity of most elder statesfolks. Everyone was shocked into admiring the forthright, unconventional way they paraded their disagreements on economic sanctions, education, domestic affairs and pottie training. In a funny way, everybody wanted to be like them. But then their constituents began to worry that the alliance they had promised wouldn't last. So I appeared, to reassure the public of their bond. On feast days and on holidays I had to be seen with them. I'd gurgle along while he led them in song from the balcony of the Great Hall, or pat my fat pink hands while she cut the ribbon on a new monument. I had a unique vantage point from where I crawled along beneath their feet. When I looked up I could see the red tinge rising from their necks to their faces as they glared at each other. I saw them twist each other's hands beneath the state table cloth. When I sat on my highchair between them at a joust or a Rotary banquet, I heard each subtly plant doubts about the other in important citizens' minds, suggestions which, if repeated before the Tribunal, could be dismissed as perfectly innocent. Both of them knew that any government which had changed the name of the Ministry of War to the Department of Defence would not take kindly to public displays of domestic first-strike capability.

As they passed me back and forth to burp me, timing their pats so I'd vomit on the other's shoulder, I heard them mutter, beneath their smiles, that some day they would blast each other off the map.

They often disrupted negotiations with practical jokes on one another. Their colleagues were amused at the apparent good-time fun of whoopee cushions on one another's seats in congress, flies floating in plastic ice-cubes in his drinks at state fêtes, garlic-flavoured chewing gum in her purse when she was on the baby-kissing circuit, the electric buzzers each wore for their hand-shake photo sessions. The papers loved reporting their youthful antics.

But I knew the terrible truth behind these jests. I knew they were only ruses. Or rather, they weren't ruses; they were meant sincerely. The morning the bomb went off in his carriage as it waited for him in front of the Great Hall, I knew who'd planted it, and who been foiled by the hangover that made him late. And when her personal secretary died of food poisoning, I knew who the potion was meant for, and who'd been foiled by Her Honour's sudden vegetarianism. I knew who was behind the wave of terrorism.

But I also wondered why, if they really wanted to off each other, they didn't.

I worried they'd plant something on me. Wire my diapers so the next person who picked me up would explode. Or fill my baby-powder dispenser with something that would choke us. I became sceptical of toys that required two to play. Before I opened my birthday presents, I listened to see if they ticked. I began to hate the notion of surprises. The quacks who stuck their doctorscopes in my ears and eyes and other places, who thumped my chest and back then tsk tsk-ed about my 'unreasonable childish fears' didn't realize that the one thing that was reasonable in the reign in which I lived was terror.

One Christmas, one of my presents under the tree was much bigger than any of the others. After I unwrapped a pair of binoculars and a neat little flashlight that fit in my hand, I picked at the tape on the ends of this huge box and, carefully, without tearing, unwrapped the shiny green and silver reindeer paper. I lifted the lid of the box and saw a 3-D picture. The background was a dainty blue sky with the lavendar hint of a sunrise, and brown-yellow reeds. Attached to the landscape by a couple of three- or four-inch-long hard, plastic bars was a foreground of ripply water. I could see some specks of paper, as thin as hair, where a machine had cut the cardboard to make it look like waves. I blew on the edges of the cardboard waves to make them clean. Sitting on top of the cardboard water were six ducks, three dark-green-headed mallard drakes and three brown-headed hens. The ducks sat in a row, boy-girl, boy-girl, equidistant from each other, their stiff profiles facing left as if they were going somewhere. They stared, one-eyed, dumb, unblinking. They looked like they would like to move from where they sat, except they couldn't. Below the water, the bottoms of their chests – they didn't have feet – were attached to the back of the cardboard by clips and springs.

The two of them impatiently lifted the picture from the box and carried it to the far end of the table. I looked in the bottom of the box and saw, resting neatly in a white moulded plastic bed, a bunch of darts and two grey plastic pistols.

They pushed the wrapping paper off the table and set up the gallery. The stiff ducks jiggled on their springs as the two of them propped the sky and water up. I sat down at the table. He yanked one of the guns from the box, she the other. They grabbed the darts. The darts were as long as my hand. Each dart had a ribbed shaft with a small hard plastic nub on one end and a flat, round rubber disc on the other. He rammed the small end of the dart into the dark open hole of his gun. The flat end stuck out. She did the same.

They both swished around me, whispering instructions about how to hold the pistol, aim, and squeeze the trigger. They hovered so close I almost felt their clothes, like spirits, sweeping me, but their black-gloved hands didn't touch me. One of them – I couldn't tell which – put a plastic pistol in my hand. My arm felt like pins and needles, then it felt nothing. The only part of my body that had any feeling, as if the feeling from each part of me had drained to it, was my hand. My hand lifted itself, like in a seance, like it wasn't mine, to eye level. I felt cool air around my finger on the trigger. My palm was moist against the tiny waffle pattern of the handle. I felt the sharp ridge of the plastic trigger beneath the pad of my fingertip.

They were impatient, almost whining, as I took aim. I felt the dull dragging on the back of my hand when the hand squeezed the trigger. I heard the pop when the trigger released the dart and the thwack of the rubber head of the dart hitting the cardboard head of the duck. The duck went down.

'Got 'im!' he whispered.

My fingers loosened slowly as if, instead of two or three seconds, my fingers had been stiffened on the gun since I was born. I wanted to drop the gun, but one of them – I couldn't tell which – caught the gun, while the other one slipped the second, loaded gun into my hand. Both of them squeezed my shoulders, their black gloves encouraging me, and whispered, 'Good, that's good.' I squeezed the trigger of the gun and got another duck. My aim was perfect. One of them reloaded the gun again and it replaced the empty one in my hand.

I watched, as if the eyes with which I saw had no relation to the hand that shot. The pins and needles feeling came back, first on the places where their gloved hands had touched me, then everywhere, until my body felt normal again. I watched as three, four, five, then all the ducks went down. 'That's good, that's good.' One of them swirled around me, touching and encouraging, while the other ran to the end of the table to set the ducks up again. I heard the pop, pop, pop as the ducks sprung back to the top of the cardboard water like they were alive. I lifted the gun and aimed.

My brother Stan was born not long thereafter.

When Stan arrived, I worried for him. By that time I'd gotten wise to some of the uses they would make of me, and how they blamed me, but Stan was a baby. I tried to warn him. I leaned over his crib and whispered to his tight shut eyes, his tiny little fists and kicking feet, 'Go back! Go back!' But he was too young to understand. Later, I held him on my knee and put my mouth to his ear and told him stories – well, lies actually – I admit it, about how much better it would be for him if he went back. They were lies because I made up the specifics, but I really did think it'd be better if he went back or if he'd never come in the first place, and that the longer he stayed, the worse it would get. But it was too late.

At the same time, I'm ashamed to admit, I was glad he was around to deflect some of the punching-bag energy they had aimed at me. In some ways, though I wanted him to grow up so I could have an ally, I didn't want him to grow up. I wanted him to stay a dumb baby long enough to keep them occupied. Maybe I wasn't really thinking of him.

But I think I was, dear Stan. I think I wanted to watch out for you. I think I wanted to for both of us.

It was not as a courtesy to one another or to me, rather a concern for efficiency that made them co-operate on the installation of a guard house in the wall. A meek old couple in hand-me-down Post Office clerk uniforms patrolled the sleepy border. My running through caused little interruption to their card game. They looked up smiling, and waved me through.

When I took the bus back and forth to the two separate government homes, I passed through the country where Stan and I used to play. Beneath the smouldering ruins of overturned tankers and smoking mines, of broken plates and coffee pots, I saw soft white covered yards, and steam rising off lakes, and brown-beige reeds, and little rays of sun that shine through clouds.

3

The Civil War

'You tell Her Grizzleship this.' He draws a couple of deep breaths and yells, 'Take your goddamned declaration of rights and shove it up your tight little frigid ass. . . .'

I memorize his words and repeat them back to him while he catches his breath. After the red has drained from his face and he's wiped the froth from his lips, I expect him to dismiss me. But he asks, 'So how is the old cow anyway?'

'Huh?' He's never asked about Her Honour before.

'Well,' he harumphs, 'you must see her when you deliver my greetings. How's she doing? Still wearing those godawful coke bottle specs? Still keeping her candy-ass cabinet in line with her school marm charm?'

'Uh . . . well . . . she's instituting a right-to-work law, um . . . a guaranteed annual income . . . mass transit . . .' I tell him only common news which he could read in any newspaper, but he doesn't read the papers. I could tell him anything I want about her and he wouldn't know what's true.

'So's the old bastard still keeping the masses down with his line about biological destiny, divine right and all that crap?'

'Huh?' I'm still scratching away at her dictation.

'C'mon, you see His Excrescence when you deliver my greetings. Does he still have that disgusting paunch? Still entertaining his greasy hoodlum fatcat buddies by oppressing the masses?'

'Um . . .' She's never asked about His Highness before. I stammer, 'Well . . . he still throws those . . . um . . . parties. I mean, sometimes I see . . . uh . . . leftovers the next day. He still seems to enjoy being a gourmet.'

'The ol' prick'll never change.' She shakes her head disapprovingly, then starts to chuckle. 'But jesus, did he know how to party.' She covers her mouth with her hand when she starts to laugh out loud. 'I remember this one soirée that was outta this world. He got these guys see . . .' But then she stops and shakes her head as if a fly were on her nose. 'God knows how much the damned thing cost.' She taps her pencil on her paper-strewn desk and snaps, 'Well, how the hell is the ol' sod?'

I tell her only common news that she could read in any paper, though I know she only reads about him rarely. She's unable to get through articles about him without throwing the paper down in disgust. I could tell her anything I want about him and she wouldn't know what's true.

I get this idea.

'I – I know some things about her you don't know.'

He glares at me over a pork chop.

Dots of colour from the stained-glass windows above me tremble on my clothes. My words rush. 'But you couldn't know anymore.'

'Oh yea, Miss Junior Uppity? Like what?'

'Well, I'm not sure.' I take a small step towards his throne. 'But if I told you, you'd know what they meant, what to do about them.'

He strokes his fat chin.

I lean close to him. I put my hands on the soft tatty weave of his chair. I peer around the Throne Room cautiously. A couple of his fat courtiers are propped back to back against each other on the floor, snoring off a night of debauchery. A guy on the couch is gurgling at a girl pinned underneath him. No one is listening to me. 'I could spy,' I whisper into his waxy ears, 'I could report back to you in secret.'

He picks his teeth, then grumbles a low growl in his throat. He sucks the last meat off his pork chop and tosses it on the floor. He smiles at me with his yellow teeth. He squeezes me on the shoulder. 'Good. That's a good idea.' Then he says, the way I like, 'That's good, that's my little girl.'

'I – I know some things about him you don't know,' I mumble.

She jabs her black-gloved index finger at me like a teacher pointing a stick. 'Honey, I've been around blocks you've never even heard of with that asshole.'

I gulp. 'New things ... um ... small changes.'

'How many times do I have to tell you there's no such thing as a small change, kid? Change only occurs with revolution, terror, blood.' She sticks her face close to mine to frighten me.

My eyes widen but I don't flinch. I grab the edge of her desk and whisper urgently, 'But there are small changes. I've *seen* them.'

She unbuttons the top button of her collar and snaps off the hidden microphone that's tacked to it. She clicks the mike off and pats the collar back neatly.

'Like what?' She raises an eyebrow.

'Well, I don't know what they mean,' I say, 'but if I told you, you'd know what to do about them.'

She presses the fingertips of her slender gloves together in front of her mouth. Her sharp grey eyes look into mine.

'I could spy,' I murmur softly. I watch my lips move in the reflection of her glasses. 'I could tell you what he does in secret.'

She runs the tips of her thumb and forefinger down the lines by her mouth. Her perfectly straight white teeth smile at me. 'Good. That's a good idea.' Then she says, the way I like, 'That's my girl. That's my little girl.'

'All well and good.' He pops an olive into his mouth. 'But what's in this for you?'

'Me?' I ask, my voice as innocent sounding as I can manage.

'Yea. You.' He spits out the pip.

'A neat job,' I say with an affected shrug. Then brightly, 'I really like adventure.'

He shakes his head slowly.

'I've always wanted to travel?' I try limply.

'Listen,' he snaps, 'I know enough about your tarnished background to know you probably have a very stunted desire for adventure. And an overdeveloped sense of safety first. And are about as trustworthy as a snake.' His eyes narrow. 'In other words, sport, you better come up with a better reason than that.'

I laugh nervously. Then I kick my instep carefully, shrug my shoulders and say, 'Jeez, I could use some allowance money.'

He pauses a moment before he guffaws. 'God knows Her Tight-Assed-ness would never pass out financial incentives. And you and I both know the best things in life aren't free, eh? Maybe you're not gonna be such a bore as I thought. Sure kiddo, let's give it a go.' He tosses me a fat leather pouch full of coins. 'That's a taste of it, sport. Plenty more where that came from – if you perform.'

'Right,' I answer, as gruffly as I can.

'So why are you doing this?'

'It's a matter of principle.' I answer firmly. After being interrogated by him, I expect this from her.

'Principle?' she snickers, 'Convince me.'

I clear my throat. 'The more I see of both sides, the more he disgusts me. I hate the degrading, patronizing, inhuman way he treats those less fortunate and those more enlightened and those even vaguely different than himself.' I hope my words will strike the right chord in her, but that she won't spot me for the shallow mouth-puppet I am. (I'm quoting almost directly from a shabbily printed pamphlet I was handed on my way across New Square.)

'Conviction is all well and good,' she grins, 'but you must, given your tainted gene pool, have something more rewarding in mind?'

I pause a couple of calculated beats, then, as if I'm being forced to admit something I'm not altogether proud of, 'Look, what's happening now is only the beginning. We're looking forward to a bloody reign of terror. And when that's over, I want to be on top.'

'With me?' she asks, almost coy.

'Yes, ma'am,' I salute, snapping my heels together.

What I will tell him someday will be this: that she has been known, after a long hard day with the senior ministers, to relax with a glass of good sherry. And sometimes these sips have not been taken alone, but rather in the company or someone or ones and that sometimes laughter and the slapping of backs has been overheard.

What I will tell her someday will be this: that he has finally, under pressure from the Surgeon Royal, cut back on fatty foods, limited his daily intake of ale, and declared portions of the Palace, while not No Smoking areas, low tar and nicotine areas. And that spot checks on danger levels of tobacco are conducted by plainclothed courtiers.

What I will tell them someday will be this, dear Stan: you have come back.

I tell them my extraordinary adaptability could give me access to secrets, to intimacies that no one will suspect. I tell them I'll be loyal and I will not leave.

But neither of them was born yesterday. They each know everybody has her breaking point, regardless of her price. So they each put me through a series of tests to find out mine. They try to see how much I can endure before I talk. They throw me into solitary, expose me to the elements, tie me in front of a bare bright bulb for hours, restrict my TV watching, deprive me of dessert, ground me from using the phone.

But I don't break, then.

They each give me a list of rules: *Do not be seen or heard. Don't tell. Don't fraternize. Do not look back. Don't use the phone. Don't ask. Do not get caught.*

'If you get caught, take this.'

Each of them gives me one individually, cellophane-wrapped, bite-sized trick or treat. Inside is a capsule; it could be a Red Hot or a Hot Tamale or a Good 'n Plenty. It's a vial of cyanide.

One needs only one. But I keep both, dear Stan.

When I pass both of their oddly similar tests, I have two small private graduation ceremonies. He cracks a bottle of bubbly over the back of the throne; she gives me a first edition of the manifesto. Each of them, sentimental with this rite of passage, says they're proud of me and calls me their little girl. This is a term of endearment both of them, despite their distance and their so-called foreign tongues, despite how hard they work at trying to forget, still have in common.

Should I have been concerned about how prepared they were to test me? It was as if they'd tested someone else before me. Shouldn't they have wondered – isn't it their own fault they didn't wonder – how adept I was at the appearance of loyalty? Or of love?

The way to succeed in the espionage business is to be someone that no one would suspect, i.e. to not be seen or heard. Medium height, medium weight and build, medium colouring, meek and mild-mannered and obedient. No visible scars, no blue or purple marks on skin, no curious tattoos. In short, to be immemorable.

His Highness gives me an advance on my allowance; Her Honour gives me some clothing ration chits. Despite the fact they call me little girl, I am a big girl now; I go out to do my clothes shopping by myself. As I leave each of their places, I grin. While neither of them acknowledges it, it's clear that each of them is trying, with whatever currency they have, to buy me.

I go to Goodwill. It's the first, original Goodwill store in the world. It has a museum. I walk in past the big, lopsided, smelly boxes of wingtips and bedroom slippers and ski-boots and high heels, straight to the damp, overstuffed racks of clothes. As I rifle through them, the pads of my fingers and my fingernails get dark. I slip my hands over bright plaid polyester shirts, dacron blouses, rayon ski-jackets. I know exactly what I want.

When I find the right things, I walk past the sagging, mildewy bookshelves to the changing cubicles. I pull the sticky shower curtain closed and strip in front of the dirty, white-streaked mirror. I drop my jeans and sweatshirt on the torn carpet. I stand in my panties and undershirt and hi-tops. My skin gets goosebumps. I'm embarrassed when I catch a glimpse of myself in the mirror, as if someone else is in the tiny room who can look at me, but it's only me. I try not to notice my skinny white legs and my knees as knobby as knots. I put one foot then the other into the big waist of the trousers. The material is slick compared to the rough texture of my K-mart imitation Levis. I grab the waist, do a little jump and yank them up. They're loose. I tighten the skinny black belt around my middle and roll up the cuffs a couple inches so they just barely cover my hi-tops. I pull the big white shirt on over my undershirt and tuck it in. When I button the top button there's a gap between it and my skin. I tie the tie. As my hands shape the slinky material into a neat knot, I suddenly remember the time when I'd taken Stan's bib off and put him in a wide black tie and made fun of how he drooled on it, and how I'd liked that they punished him, not me, for making a mess. In the mirror of the changing room I see the small white cup in the skin at the bottom of my neck. It looks so vulnerable. I shake the picture of Stan out of my head.

I shove my arms into the big sleeves of the suit jacket. The shoulders are padded. I look like a half-back. I'm glad. Looking bigger makes me feel bigger. I shake my arms and feel the material swish across my knuckles. The suit is that generic, tiny-dark-check-business-suit pattern which is grey or black or navy blue depending on the light and the tie you wear. I pull on the overcoat. The ends of its beige sleeves are slightly grey. It has big lapels which I can pull up around my head and neck in the rain and duck my face in so I won't be recognized. The coat has lots of pockets. I slide my hand inside the inner breast pocket and imagine casually pulling out a cool, silver-coloured cigarette lighter with an insignia on it. I stretch my hands way down in the deep trouser pockets where I will rattle a bunch of change and a tremendous, important-looking key ring when I get one. I pat the back of my butt as if I'm making sure I have my wallet. I stick my finger in the little pocket for the watch I want to get. I love these practical pockets that will hold and carry everything I need. I transfer the two trick-or-treat capsules from my jeans into the watch pocket.

I pick the black felt hat up from the chair and put it on my head. I lean my head back to look at myself in the mirror. I suck in a deep breath and sneer at myself. I shake my shoulders, loosen my tie, unbutton the top button of my shirt and try to look world-weary. I poke my finger into the lower corner of an outside pocket so it looks like I'm carrying a gun. I stick my other hand into another pocket and feel some limp material. I pull it out. Two black leather gloves. I look around in the changing booth to make sure no one is watching. They don't limit the number of items you can take into these rooms, or give you one of those cards that says how many items you have, but I check again in case there is a hidden camera, then slip the gloves back into the pocket.

I kick my old clothes into a corner and slip out of the changing booth. I amble through the clothing section into the Goodwill museum. I hang around casually to see if anyone notices me. I look at the Goodwill Museum collection of 1960s California ware, a bunch of old lamps, a display of a typical frontiersman's living room (wool blanket, tin cups, coal bucket, etc.). I look at a weird room full of creepy old dolls in yellow dresses, and at the Hydroplane. I read some of the articles in glass frames about the Hydroplane. No one snickers at my apparent interest in these junky discards from people's attics, the things that didn't sell at anybody's garage sale. No one taps me on the shoulder and says, 'Shouldn't you be in school this time of day, kiddo?'

I breeze through the check-out line as if I hadn't found anything. No one notices me. I'm a natural.

I cross the parking lot and walk out to Dearborn Ave. When I am out of sight of the Goodwill, I take the gloves out of my pocket and slip them on. I flex my fingers and watch the lines of the leather shift like skin. I turn my hands over and stretch my fingers so my palm is smooth as a bubble. The gloves fit perfectly.

'You look perfect,' he chortles, 'a regular pint-sized Elliott Ness.' His yellow teeth smile at me. Until he looks down at my feet. 'About those shoes. . . .'

'You look like a goddamned dream,' she grins, 'a little cloak-and-dagger Shirley Temple.' But when she looks down at my shoes, she raises an eyebrow.

I explain to each of them, in their separate homes of government, that a recent report in *Management Monthly* found that in both the public and private sector, employees who were allowed some small form of personal expression – a potted plant by the terminal, a coffee cup with their name on it in the canteen, a lucky pencil behind the ear in the steno pool, a pair of hi-tops beneath the standard uniform – were found to approach their work with more enthusiasm. In other words, these small symbolic concessions to individuality increase efficiency in the workplace.

'Balls,' she remarks.

'A load,' he explains, 'of crap.'

But when I add that, though my particular footwear might arouse the attention of conservative arbiters of espionage fashion, the shoes might also, in the unlikely event of my being caught, enable my escape, they each harumph, then grudgingly agree to let me keep my shoes for an unspecified trial period.

*
49

So I go back and forth. Over a definite, determined boundary, but also across the fuzzy lines about which there is still debate, to look for you. I walk through the electronic surveillance scanner carrying my briefcase and duty-free like normal travellers through normal lands. The border guards wave to me, unaware that I conceal a microdot beneath my fingernail, a sheet of onionskin sewn in the lining of my trench coat, the suppressed name of a boy. Or that I will return, after midnight, to tramp over a treacherous, unguarded mountain peak, or through a muddy river bed, or a steamy, bug-infested jungle. The guards don't know that some dark nights I fly overhead in a silent, unlit glider so small I can't be seen on either's radar.

But I know you can see me. Stan. You're watching.

Sometimes after he's given me a message to take to her, one of his courtiers will slur, 'Go on, offer th' kidda drink.' His Highness will hesitate, then laugh his huge round laugh and spread his arm as if he's giving the whole wide world a bearhug and slap me on the back. He'll slide me a frothy tankard and chortle, 'Fights anaemia, sport.' He'll help me lift it to my lips.

Sometimes I see his long wood table spread with dozens of heaping platters of lamb and veal, entire halves of cows. And giant loaves of sweet-smelling bread and bright yellow butter and huge round orange and white cheeses. No one ever uses napkins but wipes their hands, infrequently, on the fronts of their filthy fur vests. They all have double chins, and greasy fingers and hair. Bored-looking girls with buxom breasts pressed tight in low-cut dresses sit on fat guys' laps. I once saw a girl eating a drumstick while a pock-faced old guy pawed her tits. Sometimes the excess of all this almost sickens me, but I never turn down what he offers me. Despite the unfair opulence, I like his spread more than the watery soup and slices of unbuttered bread she says I ought to be grateful for.

Sometimes when he's had more than a few, he'll sniff and ask, 'No really, how is the silly old cow? Doesn't she miss me?'

Each of them has strict laws forbidding trade or commerce across the border. They both say it's treason; it will end in a terrible death.

She outlaws all things she calls frivolous, luxurious, all things unique to his kingdom. She says they are unhealthy, that contact with any one of them will throw one into sickness unto death. She declares that anyone who happens to escape by a medical oddity is a traitor and will be shot before the public.

I steal a frivolous luxury from his table, like a mango or papaya. I conceal it in a pocket and carry it across the border to her land. I don't take it to sell it or to show it off or even to tempt some gullible person to join me. And certainly not because I have an uncontrollable craving for illicit things. I do it to see if I can. When I'm alone I take it out and look at it. I bite into it. Nothing happens. It tastes OK, but not such great shakes it needs to be outlawed. I bite into it in public, on the flagstone plaza. No one notices.

On the way to the Palace, in a pocket, along with my tapes and papers, I carry a copy of her manifesto which he's declared blasphemous. He's said that anyone touching it, if not immediately stricken dead by God, will be beheaded by His Highness personally. I run my finger below the lines as I read it silently, but I am left alone by God. When I'm kept waiting outside the Throne Room, I hold it in front of me like the daily paper, but no one notices. When I rustle it in my pocket as I'm standing in front of His Highness, he doesn't react.

The terrible things they say about each other, Stan, their threats, are lies. If I could march right up to each of them and show them what I've brought across, a soft-skinned fruit, a piece of paper, and say, 'You've lied,' would they admit it?

I know I lied to them, dear Stan, but I lied with the purest of intents. I lied for I believed with all the things that warred in me that the war between the two of them was a civil one, that given time and my diplomacy, could be undone. And I believed, dear Stan, and I still do, despite what's come of all my well-intentioned, altered truths, about the necessary means to ends. I lied because I knew that each of them with their ruthless talk of principle, their terrible ability to murder what they can't control, would never be willing to compromise, or say they're sorry, would never agree to undo what they had done. I lied because I thought a lie would bring you back, dear Stan.

I work so hard. I work all the time. It's rare that I'm not working on an assignment. When I do have time off, I usually travel to some exotic place like Rio, Istanbul, Seattle, because any place I go may come in handy, any place may have a clue about the whereabouts of you, dear Stan.

But sometimes when I just want to rest, I show up at the border house and tap on the kitchen window. One of the old guards will shuffle to the window to see it's me, then shuffle to the door and let me in. After I've stayed with them a few times, though, I just tap on the window so they see me, then let myself in the door. They don't mind. They never lock their door. They don't have anything worth taking. Besides, all the other cowering citizens on both sides of the wall believe the terrible things Her Honour and His Highness say will happen to anyone unauthorized who dares approach the border.

Actually, the old border guards don't have much of a purpose. Perhaps they take notes about my passing and report back to Him and Her that I've done my assignment on time, but they aren't really needed.

Sometimes I think about how these old guys are in such a great position; they could overthrow everything. They're right there in the centre, and, as much as anybody, trusted by both of them. They could organize and recruit. If I was in their position. I'd start a party. I'd stockpile guns, stage a rally, a crusade, a full-scale revolution. I'd sabotage the bus. But the old guards just shuffle and say, 'Yes, Your Honour,' 'Yes, Your Highness.' They never talk back. I don't respect how they've succumbed. I don't really take them seriously.

I don't see them taking each other seriously either. All they seem to do is sit at their kitchen table and play cards or politely ignore each other as they putter around their garden. On a good day, they shuffle out; on a bad one, they stumble out on their walkers or canes. They creak over their sharp-smelling tomato plants, their lowlying squash and watermelon vines. They pull up tiny radishes and carrots. They prune their lilacs and violets and forget-me-nots and pansies. Their tools aren't shiny, their gloves aren't clean. The fingertips and palms of their canvas gloves are shiny with wear. Sometimes they pick little bugs off stems with their bare, skinny hands. Their hands have purplish spots. The hand-me-down Post Office clerk uniforms they always wear sag around their bodies. Sometimes their heads nod for no reason at all. They don't have teeth. Their cheeks go in and their lips are thin and pale. Their hair is wispy and yellow-white.

After I've stayed at their cottage a few times, I ask them about the civil war, but they don't seem to have much opinion. They nod when I tell them what I think. But when I present, for the sake of argument, a completely different view, they mutter agreeably, 'Well, yes, there's that as well. . . .' When they shake their heads back and forth, it isn't to disagree, but to croak with sympathy, 'Oh dear, isn't that a shame . . .'

Neither of them seems particularly happy with the way things are. When I, for example, suggest that both governments run covert terrorist operations, and flagrantly abuse human rights, neither of them defends Her Honour or His Highness. And neither of them says they're going to do anything about it.

Once I asked them if anyone else had ever come through the border. They both lowered their heads and shrugged. 'Was it a boy,'

I hammered, but they didn't answer me. One of them made a transparent excuse about needing to tend to something in the garden. Then they both went out and I heard the soft, slow sounds as they loosed and turned the dirt.

But I kept staying with them, from time to time, when I wanted rest. I helped them to do things they couldn't do alone. I put up a trellis and dug some post holes. I hauled piles of broken concrete and rocks and I whitewashed the house. Once when I was working really hard, really working up a sweat, I turned around and saw her looking at me. I couldn't tell if it was gratitude or envy that I still had the strength to do these things, or something else. I bent back down and started really tearing through it, yanking up dandelions and clover and flinging it in the air like a machine. I looked up again because I felt her right over me, watching me. The sun was very bright around the outline of her body. 'Don't,' she said in that weak, wimpering voice of hers, 'Please don't.' I was going to tell her not to worry, that I'd clean it all up when I was done, but just then he stuck his head out the kitchen window and said he'd made us some lemonade, so we went back inside and drank it.

Every time I stood on the door step of the cottage to leave, they'd say, 'Do you have to leave?' even though they knew I could only stay a while. They'd hand me a sack lunch they'd made and say, 'Come back,' as if they thought I wouldn't. They'd wave goodbye to me with their pale, little, flag-like squares of hankies. On the bus I'd unpack the lunch. Thick sandwiches on home-made bread with cheese and mayonnaise, or peanut butter and jelly they'd jarred themselves. Bread and butter pickles from their own cucumbers, a slice of apple pie. Hard little red-orange peaches from their peach tree.

His Highness winks at me, wags his black-leather finger towards himself. I step up on the dais to him. He grabs my hand and pulls me to him. 'You're getting to be a big girl, little girl.' His voice is throaty. My skin feels like it's shrinking. He glances over my shoulder to make sure the Throne Room is empty. Then he yanks me behind the dais. His arm is around my neck. I feel my shoulder pressed against his chest. He slaps his hand over my mouth. His other hand pulls a fat leather-bound book off the Top Secret Bookshelf. I hear a creak and suddenly the small semi-circle of floor we're standing on spins into a concealed chamber. My skin is wet, my pulse is racing. He pushes me away from him. I fall forward, my clammy hands swimming in the dark. The room smells musty and sweaty. I gather the Palace cleaning ladies don't get back here very often. I hear a zipping noise; he's lit a candle. I'm grateful for the smell of the struck match. When I turn back to face him, the candle lights his fat face up. His face looks pale and oily like something awful that lives underground. His fat, many-ringed fingers cup around the light, protecting it from a chilly draft.

'We're gonna throw the ol' cunt for a helluva loop,' he snickers. He sticks his hand in his tights beneath his long shirt. My throat feels like I'm going to spit as I listen to him fiddle. In a couple seconds he brings his hand out from his shirt. He's holding something I can't see. 'She won't be able to tell the difference between this and the real thing.' He explains to me that I'm to plant a false 'secret' where she'll find it and be misled. He drops a cassette into my open palm.

'Yessir.' I squint down at the frosty plastic case, the black circle of tape inside. It's hard to see in the dim room. I drop the tape into one of my raincoat pockets.

'Here's your instructions where to drop it,' he snorts, 'and your allowance.' He slaps a wilted, sweaty envelope into my hand. I shove it into my pocket. 'And while you're over there,' he pauses, then gets this overly matter-of-fact lilt to his voice, 'drop this off. My other kid behind the lines will pick it up.'

I catch my breath, but try to cover my surprise – who is this other kid? – with an efficient, 'Yessir.'

He drops the second cassette, almost indistinguishable from the first, into my palm. I give the second tape a puzzled glance then drop it into another raincoat pocket.

'Here's your instructions for that.' He chuckles, slapping another wilted envelope into my hand, 'and a little bonus.' I can barely see the bills and the sheet of typewriter paper inside. I wait a couple of seconds to see if he has more to tell me.

It gets darker when he moves towards me. His bulky body blocks the thin light. I can't see anything, but I feel his slick gloves on the sides of my neck. I feel my skin move when I swallow. My gurgles sound very loud in this cramped room. One of his hands grips the back of my cold, sweaty neck; the other turns me around. I close my eyes and clench my teeth, hoping I can keep myself from gagging. I hear a slipping sound behind me. My hands are trembling inside my pockets. I feel him take a step towards me. His body is against my back. In front of me is the wall. His hot, wet breath is on my neck. He snickers. He knows I'm terrified. I hear a slick, shifting sound. Suddenly, white shoots into my eyes. They spring open.

It's light; he's opened the wall in front of me. He pushes me back into his Throne Room. I trip. He holds me up by my armpits and laughs. When my legs can hold me up again, he releases me. He slaps me on the back and smiles. Bits of green and black things are stuck in his teeth.

I scurry across the wooden floor of the throne room to the ante-chamber door. I tuck my head down into my upturned collar. My tennies squeak.

'And do something about those goddamned tennis shoes fergod-sake!' he yells behind me.

I feel myself blush as I try to hike my too-long trousers up around my waist and step more quietly. I look up when I hear his heavily mascaraed, very sexy clerk giggle at me. I blush hotly, and hurry out to the courtyard.

He's given me two sets of instructions, two maps to different parks, two tapes.

Do I even have to tell you, Stan, that I get another pair from her?

Should I be concerned, once again, at the unlikely similarities of their plans?

I tell myself the likeness of their methods is due to their common backgrounds. I tell myself the very fact that they share the same susceptibilities, the same deceptions, shows that they are meant to be each other's partner. I'm right to work to bring them back. Like you, dear Stan, I have been born and bred for this.

His Highness' instructions say to drop the tape in a standard, sand-wich-sized, brown-paper sack in a particular garbage can by a particular bench by the zoo in People's Park. The pencil-drawn map has a spot marked 'x'. I'm to memorize the map, then eat it. I've got to supply the brown-paper sack myself.

I take a bus to People's Park. It's mid-afternoon, a nice, warm sunny weekday. Most people are at school, but the bus is pretty full. A bunch of old folks sit near the centre of the bus in their Sunday best. They are all very tidy. Their purple, age-splotched hands rest neatly on their laps or knees or occasionally on one another's hands. They've all tucked their compact, old-fashioned overnight cases under their seats, careful not to take up more than their share of room. They chat quietly, happily, with one another while a couple of them pass around xeroxed sheets of paper. When they read these sheets, their lips move silently and their heads gently bob in rhythm. And all of the old folks, whether toothless, or with dentures or with crooked grey teeth of their own, are smiling.

The only other people on the bus are a few older kids watching babies. I slouch in my trench coat and hat behind the newspaper hoping no one will ask me why I'm not in school. I peer over the top of the paper through half-slit eyes.

Some of the kids start pointing and the babies start screeching and squirming and flapping their fat little arms. The old folks and I look out the windows. We're going by the zoo. Over the tops of a well-kept hedge, I can see the cream-coloured, gawky necks of giraffes, the high-as-a-cathedral net of the aviary, and monkeys swinging from trees. Some of the old folks lean to their neighbours and say very loudly, 'It's – the – zoo. The – children – are – excited – about – the – zoo.' Some of the old guys make corny jokes about 'monkey business', while others smile sweetly or give those wide, exaggerated smiles adults give to babies. No one has to dink the bus stop request wire. The driver knows when to stop. He raises his hands and stretches his legs out in the aisle, knowing it will take a while for the kids to alight. Some of the old guys insist on helping the girls with the strollers crammed full of blankets and plastic toys and cartons of paper diapers and picnic food. Older babies toddle off in sandals and shorts, dragging fuzzy teddy bears and dolls by the ankles behind them. I get off the bus too, but don't get to follow them to the zoo.

As the bus pulls away I see some of the old folks waving goodbye to the bright-eyed kids and babies. One of the old folks waves to me. I start to wave back, but remind myself: *Do not be seen or heard.* I stuff my hand in my pocket. But the bus pauses, as if to let this old guy keep waving his smudgy hand at me. He smiles this wide open smile, then moves his mouth, saying something to me. Of course I can't hear, but I look at him. My arm feels like pins and needles, like it isn't mine. Partly my arm lifts itself, and partly it's me, knowing what I'm doing, but doing it anyway; I'm lifting my hand to wave at the old guy. When he and I stop waving, the bus moves on. I yank my arm down and look around to make sure no one's seen me. I duck my head in my collar and slouch across the street.

There's a sleazy cigarette and newspaper store on the corner. Inside it's dark and smells like the refrigerated cigarette smoke air in a motel room. In a gargly, fake eastern-European accent, I ask the pimply guy behind the cash register for a Reeses. He pauses a second. With exaggerated courtesy he picks a package up from right beneath my nose.

'Oooops—' I squeak.

I jangle around in my pockets and fish out some change. I turn away from him as I look at the different coins. I bite my lower lip trying to remember how many of which make thirty. I gulp, tuck my face deeper into my collar and turn back to him. I stand on tiptoes, stick my hand up to him and shrug. Carefully, as if he were picking a bug up off the floor, he lifts three small silvery coins and drops them in the till. Then he drops the candy into my hand. I shift back and forth from one sneaker to the other. He presses down on the counter with his fleshy palms. I watch his biceps twitching under the rolled-up sleeves of his black T-shirt.

'Bag?' I growl, shaking the candy at him as threateningly as I can.

'Ya wanna bag fer that?' His pimply forehead crinkles when he raises his eyebrows.

I tug my hat down further over my nose and nod.

He grumbles under his breath as he leans under the counter to get me a bag. I try to take it from his hand, but he pulls back.

'Not until I see some manners.' He's suddenly very patronizing.

'Thanks,' I mumble into my collar, trying hard to not be seen or heard. I reach for the bag again, but he lifts it high above me.

'Pardon me,' he asks with the cruel politeness of an over-educated villain in a cheap horror movie. 'I don't believe I heard you. You need to speak up.'

It's always when I'm trying to be neither seen nor heard that somebody asks me to speak up; and when I want to talk they shut me up.

'Thank you,' I repeat clearly. I stand on my tiptoes and stretch towards the bag.

He takes a step backwards, away from me. 'Thank you – ?' he pauses, grinning.

'Thank you, Sir.'

'You're very welcome,' he says prissily. But he still doesn't give it to me. He waves it above his head, teasing me, and gets this pouty look on his face as he looks down at me. 'Why do you need this little baggie so much, little girl?'

I spring like I'm making a jump shot at centre court – these hi-tops are good for something – and snatch the bag from him. I shove the Reeses in it as I spin around and dash out to the street. I hoof it to the sidewalk and start to run across but I'm stopped by a hand on my shoulder. It's a doddering old crossing guard. He's waving a glow-in-the-dark orange and white traffic flag and putting his arm around me to help me cross. I shake my shoulder out from him and stomp across. He shuffles along behind me, barely able to keep up. I know the top of my black fedora probably only comes to his shoulder, but I wish he wouldn't try to treat me like what I am.

When we've crossed over to the other side of the road, he produces a wax-paper-wrapped sandwich from inside his hand-me-down Post Office uniform. He pats me on the head and wishes me a cheery 'Good luck!' I spin away without even glancing at him.

Sweat trickles down the armpits of my heavy coat. I stand in the muggy shade of an oak tree overhanging the park gate. I take the Reeses out of the bag and drop the bag in my pocket. I tear open the orange and yellow and brown wrapper and crumple it into my pocket. I look at the two chocolate discs on the cardboard slat. Their neat cupcake-paper edges are limp from the heat. My fingers smudge with chocolate as I peel the ribbed paper off. I pop one of the Reeses in my mouth. I suck on it a few seconds then break it against the roof of my mouth with my tongue. I press it to the roof of my mouth and feel the gritty texture of the peanut butter. In a few seconds I feel the sweetness and thickness melting down the back of my throat.

I look down at the cardboard slat on which the other Reese is resting. They package these Reeses the way they do Mounds or Twinkies or Ho-Hos so you can share one with the partner you go halfies with, or if you don't have a partner, so you can save one for later. Later, like someday, is that indefinite time in the future when things held off till then will somehow, magically, be better.

Behind the gate, I hear the happy companionable grunts and chirps and squacks of animals and kids and babies inside. I look down at the other Reeses. I'm sure I'll find you someday, Stan, but I don't know when. I pop the other Reeses in my mouth.

I look left and right to see no one is watching, then rearrange the mess in my pocket. I open the paper sack and drop a cassette in. Then, on top of it, the candy wrapper, cupcake papers and cardboard. I squash the top of the bag closed so it looks like an ordinary ball of trash. Reminding myself that the little hand is hours and the big one is minutes, I pull my watch out of my watch pocket and step into the park.

It's a perfect green park, the grass as short and smooth as His Highness' tennis court. The individual blades of grass are thin, but so dense it feels thick when you sit in it. Or so I imagine as I look wistfully at the kids and babies sprawled out on blankets surrounded by plastic brown-nippled bottles and compact grey-white squares of Tupperware, plaid thermoses. Babies crawl around in bright-white diapers and soft pastel shirts and booties. The kids bustle around rearranging the stuff on the blankets. Some of the bigger babies try to meander off, but are called back by their watchful older siblings.

Head tucked, I hurry by the picnickers to the other side of the park. I measure my steps to the bench marked on the map. No one is sitting on the bench. I try to amble casually, but my heart races. I reach into my pocket for the paper sack. The paper crackles so loudly I almost jump. I drop the sack into the garbage can beside the bench.

I keep walking, but I am very, very curious about the other guy who's supposed to pick the package up. *Do not look back*, I recite to myself. *Don't fraternize. Don't ask.* But when I get to the end of the path I pause and, pretending I'm only trying to see what the noise is, look back. Far off, from the other side of the park, come high-pitched squeals, excited shouts and concerned deeper orders, 'Don't leave! Get back here! We're about to start!' It sounds like they're organizing a game. A whistle blows. I can barely see, through the shaggy hedge dividing us, a great party of kids. Surreptitiously, I glance over at the path to the garbage can again to see if someone is coming to get the tape; there's no one.

I start to leave. I drop my head into my upturned collar, slouch my shoulders and shove my hands into my pockets. That's when I feel the tape: I've delivered the wrong tape.

I spin back to look at the garbage can. Suddenly, a shaky wino has appeared from nowhere. I don't know if it's a real wino or maybe its the other spy wearing a wino get-up. I duck behind a bush to watch him. The wino mumbles to himself in gibberish, at least that's what it sounds like. I strain to hear if he is actually transmitting coded messages to a miniature microphone hidden on his person. I can't make out anything besides nonsense syllables.

He bumps into the bench, swears loudly, then lurches over to the garbage can. He sways as he looks into it. I stare at the back of his oversized beige raincoat. He starts tossing curled orange rinds, Dr Pepper cans, paper cups, wet newspapers out of the can. He hoists out a big styrafoam take-out plate. He teeters back to the bench and plops down to examine the pickings.

He hasn't found my paper sack.

I watch the guy eat with dirty, nicotine-stained fingers. He slops through the plate like a baby eating mudpies. I can't imagine my partner in espionage would assume such a degrading get-up.

The branches of the bush I crouch behind scratch me. I'm just about to stand up and walk back to the trash can and trade the tapes when I see someone else coming down the path. Medium height, medium build, hands shoved in the pockets of a too-big beige raincoat not unlike mine.

I push the branches aside to look closer. I can't see the kid's features beneath his dark hat pulled down over his face. The kid walks past the wino with only a glance at the plate in his lap and pauses in front of the trash can. Very subtly, he glances to either side of himself, stands on his tiptoes, revealing the backs of his hi-tops, leans into the trash can, and retrieves the sack I had dropped.

Leaves scratch my face as I leap from behind the bush. 'Hey, watch out—'

He spins around when he hears my voice.

'That's the wrong message!'

He's clutching the sack to his chest with a blue-splotched hand.

'Stan!'

He shoves the sack into one of his raincoat pockets and runs.

I jump from the bushes. 'Don't leave!' I scream.

My shoes pound on the path as I huff along behind him. He tears through the shaggy hedge. On the other side of the hedge are hundreds – no – thousands of children. The older ones are trying to stretch the well-behaved, hand-holding younger ones into a circle for Ring Around the Rosie. But most of the kids are making mayhem on their own. A bunch of big boys run up on little girls and boys from behind, throw their arms around them and blow screeching whistles in their ears, then run off leaving fallen lumps of shocked kids on the ground. A few nasties have climbed into trees to bomb others below. What must have been a baseball game has degenerated into a bean-ball session. Two tough girls chase each other around swinging base-ball bats. Some huge greasy haired guys tromp on picnic baskets, kick over drinks, tear up boxes of diapers and smash toys. A small gang squats over a poker game and smokes, while others play doctor with a couple of screaming tied-down little babies. The small pink ones in diapers, too shocked to cry, just stand around looking lost.

I see, weaving between the terrible kids, the guy in the raincoat. I try to follow him, but the careful, skinny path he carves closes behind him. A bunch of kids about my height press around me. I can smell the dusty kid smell of their hair and skin, the ears they haven't washed behind. I can't breathe.

'Lemme go!' I scream. 'I can't let him leave. I gave him the wrong—'

But either they don't listen, or mind, or my pathetic plea doesn't move them, because the more I struggle, the more they squeeze me in. They kick me with their sneakers. Two of them grab my hands and push me down. A few jump on to my back. As I start to crumble, I see their leering faces level with mine, then above me their open mouths.

'Stan!' I cry. The kids push me down. One girl presses her foot against my neck.

I know Stan's running to escape from them, but I scream to him. 'Don't leave!'

But Stan did not come back.

I don't know if they left me for dead but they left me.

The park is empty. I sit up slowly. My body feels like one big bruise. I gingerly remove my gloves and feel the blood and mud caked on my puffy face. My raincoat is torn. My shirt is ripped and my trousers and panties are down around my ankles. I'm glad I can't remember what they did to me. I feel around in my pockets for my trick-or-treat capsules, but they're gone. As is the junk I was supposed to deliver; I've lost it.

I feel my ribs and legs. Nothing seems broken. I pull my clothes back on as much as I can and stand up carefully. I start to walk but I don't know where to go. I hobble over to a bench and look out at the park. It's a humid night. The grass is perfect, not a sign that anyone has been trampled. A fine silver coat of light is on everything.

'Stan?' I say to the warm humid air, 'Stan?'

If I'd not left, it would have been a different night. The TV would be buzzing in the den behind me. One of them behind me would say, 'Go call your brother back,' and I'd step out to the porch.

I'm on the porch looking down the street. I hear the quiet, even whht-whht-whht of sprinklers spreading circles of tiny dots of water on our neighbours' yards. I lift my head, put my half-opened hand to my cheek, open my mouth and shout, 'Staaa-aaan!' The only thing I hear is the whht-whht-whht. I take a breath and shout again, 'Staaan-leeey!' I think I hear an echo from the last part of his name. I lower my hand and hear the sound of the sprinklers, the creak of someone's car door, the whack of a porch screen door. Suddenly there are goose bumps on my arms. I watch the street fade, like television, from the greens and reds and yellows of grass and cars and lawn chairs to black and silver and grey.

Everything sounds like it's waiting. Then there's a tentative buzz, like a question, like an orchestra warming up, then the full round sound of a million crickets. Apricot-coloured lights go on in grey houses. Dingy beige curtains close in black square walls, the butterscotch glow of living-room lights inside them.

'Staaan-leeey!'

Then I hear it, very faint, so soft I could be just imagining it, until it separates, rising above the crickets' hum. It gets louder, I hear each part of it clearly, the slap of the toe on the rubber sole, the fall of the arches and

heels. I hear the huff of his breath, its eagerness and weariness. I hear the
swish of his shorts against his skinny thighs.

Then in the darkness I see flashes of white light, like a fish underwater
at night. I hear the thump of his shoes on the bottom step of the porch, the
rasping of his lungs. I feel his moist skinny arms around my back, his
heaving chest. I feel the flutter against my stomach, my brother's beating
heart.

I'm on the bus. I'm the only passenger. I don't know where I'm going.
I feel the hum of the tyres on a smooth, flat road. I try to settle in
the seat so my body feels fewest of its bruises. Outside the window,
everything is dark except the thin white spears of the headlights that
go in front of us on the cool grey snake of the road. I look out of both
sides of the bus and gradually, almost like it's rising up, materializing, I
see a faint hint of dusty brown, of plains that sweep to mesas. If I
could see more, I think I might see stars, the moon, a light.

I can't see who is driving the bus. When I lean out into the aisle
and look through the frosted glass panel that divides the driver from
the main part of the bus, I see a silhouette, the brim of a hat. If I
look long enough, I see a glove slide over the rim of the wheel loosely,
confidently, as if whoever drives this bus has driven this route many
times before.

The bus lets me off in front of the Palace. I limp to the Throne
Room trying to hold my shirt and trousers closed with my hands.

'You look like hell!' His Highness laughs. 'What'd I miss?'

When I open my mouth, no words come out.

'That good?' he chortles, stepping down from his dais with open
arms. 'Well, kiddo, welcome to the world!' He slaps me on the back
like a cronie. I wince. 'Now that you've been around the big bad
block—' he gives me a knowing wink, 'you may be ready for some
new kind of work. Besides—' he yanks the torn lapel of my coat,
'these duds are looking kind of beat.'

I nod but even a movement as slight as this shoots pain through
my body. I topple backwards and fall down in a faint.

When I come to, I'm lying on a pile of furs in a huge room I've
never been in before. I blink.

'Sleep it off, tiger?'

'I guess,' I answer groggily.

'How 'bout a hair of the dog?'

'No!' I shout, clutching the front of my shirt tightly.

His eyes widen in genuine surprise. 'Hey – sorry.' He holds both
gloved hands up and backs off like I'm being overly sensitive. He

really does look innocent. I truly think it doesn't occur to him that my roughing-up results from anything other than my latent party-girl wildness. He can't imagine that someone would dishevel me without at least my ultimate consent. He can't imagine I wouldn't want what he thinks is good for me.

I sit on a pile of furs and look out of a tall skinny window. We're several floors up. I look down on a maze and a formal garden. Sharp hedges outline boxes of bright red and purple flowers. Some of the trees are cut like animals. There's an enclosed herb garden and tennis lawn and a moat. I've never noticed when I've run up and down the poplar-lined approach, the shimmering gold fields dotted with sheep and bundles of hay and shepherds and farmers and falconers. I see a few scattered charred foundations of burnt-down houses, but otherwise, very little sign of the civil war. The forests fuzz into the distant horizon of the border.

'Nice spread, eh?' He addresses me quietly, like a peer, a minion.

'Yea . . .'

'As long as we can keep Cunty-paws off it.' He clears his throat. I turn around to face him. 'Look, I'm a little concerned she might be getting wise to you. I've had reports – never mind from who-the-hell – that you've been spotted.' He picks at something in his ear with his black-gloved pinkie. 'Seems you may have made something of a display of yourself in a candy shop?'

'I – I didn't say anything.'

He shrugs. 'These things happen, pal. You just need some new get-ups.'

Somehow it seems he's letting me off easier than he should.

He hoists himself over to a huge oak chest, fetches a skeleton key from the important-looking key chain hidden beneath his paunch. When the chest creaks open, I get a whiff of musty old clothes.

'God I love this,' he bubbles. He rips his feathered cap off and tosses it carelessly across the room. He swishes through the trunk, pulls out a huge white wig and puts it on. A stray coil of hair hangs down his back. He turns around to face me, smoothing the wrinkles out of a red and gold brocade dress. He holds the dress up to himself, points one toe to the ground, turning this knee to the other, lowers a shoulder, thrusts his hip forward and asks in a waitress-with-a-beehive voice, 'Whadya think, honey?'

When he winks at me, I blush. 'I – I—'

He lets out a huge laugh and tosses the dress and wig at me. The gold threads scratch my swollen hands.

'Loosen up a little, toots.'

He reaches into the chest again and pulls out a crown of laurels. 'Now this baby, this is the real friggin' McCoy.' He pulls the crown on to his head, turns sideways, sucks his gut in, places one foot slightly before the other, crosses his fist over his chest and lifts his chin. 'Think I'd pass?'

I clutch the brocade dress as if I could hide in it, and shake my head slightly.

'How 'bout the profile?' He sticks his nose up in the air.

'Bigger,' I suggest meekly.

He puts an outstretched thumb above his lip and stretches a fore-finger up to his forehead to make an outline of a bigger nose.

I sit up. 'That's better....'

One hand still over his nose, he turns to face me. He sweeps the other hand like an orator, and in an absurdly deep voice, recites. 'Frrrrriends, Rrrrromans—' He raises his eyebrows at me like a ten-year-old, and snickers, 'and dickheads.'

My ribs hurt when I force out a single, 'Ha!'

He claps his hands like the class clown, finally happy to have cracked the last kid's smile.

'Try this.' He tosses me a slinky red jump suit with a pointed black tail. 'Or this—', a long black Cleopatra wig and sandals. 'I know it isn't you, sport, but give it a try—'

His Majesty and I play dressing up. He gently helps me pull the tops over my head and shoulders, but he doesn't look. He turns away discreetly while I change my bottoms. He zips the backs I can't reach. He's careful not to touch my cuts or bruises. He pats my hair and shoulders, tilting his head like a hairdresser. 'That's not quite right ... there ... ooooh that's you, doll, that's really you.'

He paints our faces with brightly coloured, oily sticks of make-up. His leather gloves get smudged but he doesn't remove them as I do mine. He imitates, like an impish adolescent, the walks of pompous soldiers, sycophantic courtiers, and waddling priests. We talk in lisps and silly accents and wave our hands like generals, musicians, ballerinas.

How much of my laughter is release, I don't know. I haven't told him, or anyone, what had really happened to me. But as I laugh, my bruises and cuts stop stinging.

The room is a wreck when we leave, giggling, down the hidden spiral staircase some time past midnight. We know, but like a couple of spoilt brats, we don't care, that the overworked Palace cleaning ladies will have to pick our mess up after us. We sneak into the Great Kitchen to raid it. We gnaw cold turkey legs and pies and sausages and chocolate cake and raisin buns and oatmeal cookies and cold spaghetti. He dashes off to the beer cellar and returns with as many big dark bottles as he can carry. We start a contest to see who can burp the loudest until we realize we'll probably wake someone, and we don't want anyone interrupting our party.

We collapse on the floor, our backs to the cool white walls, and pass the last brown bottle back and forth. Gradually, our shoulders lean towards each other, then our heads. By the time our silly chatter has turned to snores, our bodies rest, propping each other up.

Sometime in the night, I wake to find him wheezing, open-mouthed like a baby. His heavy arms have fallen on me, his body half faces mine. I look at his slightly parted lips that open to the dark inside of him. I watch his eyelids flicker as if I can read his dreams. I feel the warmth of his body through his clothes. Carefully, so I won't wake him, I pick his hand up. With the tips of my index finger and thumb, I lift the edge of the wrist of his glove and look inside at his hand. Maybe it's too dark to see, or maybe I am dizzy with drink, but I think I see small dots of colour on his hand.

The next morning when I leave, I leave reluctantly. But I have learned enough from both of them to know how to hide my second thoughts.

He slumps in his throne. I stand before him and clear my throat. He doesn't say anything.

'What should I tell her?' My voice is cold.

'Huh?' He starts as if his mind is somewhere else.

'The message.' My voice is clipped. 'I'm here to take her a message.'

He blinks at me, trying to focus. He's dressed me in pointy shoes and a jerkin and a pair of skinny old tights he wore as a boy. He steps off the throne to brush some imaginary lint from my shoulder. He walks around me and fusses with my clothes. I stare straight ahead.

'What am I to tell her?'

'Oh, the usual . . .' he puffs up my slashed sleeves.

I clear my throat and repeat severely. 'What am I—'

He grabs me by my shoulders and snaps, 'Tell her the usual goddamn thing you tell her every goddamn time you leave!' He yanks his hands away from me like he's just touched something hot.

I flinch.

'Goddammit – just make it up as you go along. You've goddamn done it before—' He glares at me then stomps back to his throne. 'Forget it. Just get out of here. Leave.'

I hesitate.

'*Leave.*'

My sleeves swish when I walk away from him.

'You look ridiculous,' she says before I've even started to improvise his message. 'Where the hell did you get that asshole get-up?'

I look down at the tights bagging around my ankles, the toes that curl up in points, my gloves tucked into my belt. I quickly clasp my smudged hands behind my back where she can't see them. I shrug, pretending I'm just as surprised as she.

She eyes me silently.

'I was worried I was starting to get recognized . . .'

'Balls.' She pushes her chair back and marches around to the front of the desk. She clasps her gloved hands neatly in front of her lap. 'Next time you want to make any goddamned changes in the programme you talk to *me*.' What she states is not an order; it's a fact.

'Yes ma'am.'

She pushes her glasses up on her nose. She eyes me from head to toe. 'We will now attempt to restore whatever scrap of respectability we may be able to.' She snaps her fingers for me to follow her. She presses a button inside a desk drawer and a wall opens up behind her. A thin grey staircase leads down. I take a few steps after her. Behind me the door clangs shut.

'You breathe a word of this to anyone, you're meat. You hear that?'

'Yes ma'am.'

I stick my hands out in front of me like a blind person. She snatches my hands and pulls me down the stairs behind her. I trip. When I pick myself up I'm on solid ground at the bottom of the stairs. There's a click when she turns on the light.

'Holy shit,' I whisper. 'Hooo-leeeeey shit. Where did you get all this – shit?' That's the only word for it.

We're in a pink flower wall-papered dream-girl's bedroom from a bygone era: pastel-pink dresser with vanity mirror and make-up light, a bunch of sappy black-and-white posters of classically good-looking, full-lipped male movie stars, penants from State U., a rose-coloured princess telephone, canopy bed with dotted swiss-pink coverlet, a hot-pink plastic trash can, a pink feather duster. A door opens off the room where I see a pink fuzzy toilet cover, a pink plastic shower curtain, pink hairbrush and toothbrush and a pink designer holder for dental floss. And, as a precautionary measure, a bottle of pink Pepto-Bismol on the sink.

'Siddown,' she orders, pushing me into a hot-pink beanbag chair. She stomps over to the closet, slides back the pretty-boy-poster-covered door, and stretches her plain brown-suited arm up to the top shelf. She rattles around for a bit. 'Help me get this down,' she commands.

I scramble up out of the chair and step over to the closet. On the top shelf are two couple-feet-long flat paper-and-wire sculptures.

'Careful,' she whispers, suddenly tender.

I stand on my tiptoes and take the pointed end of one of them. The paper feels brittle and old. I walk backwards as she coerces the awkward upper part of the closet. We carry it over to the bed then get the other one.

'We'll start with this,' she says self-consciously. 'Hope it still fits . . .' She sits on the edge of the bed and folds her hands demurely in her lap. 'Um . . . you'll um . . . need to remove your clothing,' she says shyly.

Modestly, I turn my back to her to slip out of my jerkin.

As soon as I've lowered the shoulders, she gasps. I turn around to see she's standing up, hands over her mouth, her wide eyes looking at my scratched, bruised skin.

'Oh dear god, what happened to you—' she chokes.

'I'm better now,' I start to explain. But I don't want to admit that I was caught on a mission to double-cross her.

'Oh my god,' she breathes again. 'I was always afraid this would happen to you. I always knew he'd do this.' She covers her face with her hands and sits back down on the bed in a daze.

'It wasn't—' I almost correct her, but I don't. Because she's awkwardly trying to put her arm around me, to comfort me. I can tell she isn't used to touching people. I pull her arm around me and lean into her lapels. She smells like furniture oil.

'You poor thing,' she says, 'you poor, poor baby.'

I know it's cheating to let her comfort me for something that didn't happen the way she thinks it did, but I want her to.

We murmur comforting-sounding nonsense syllables to one another. Gradually her arms hold me more easily.

'I want you to quit this,' she sniffs, her soft gloves on my cheeks. 'I don't want you to go back there. I don't want you to ever have to see that terrible—' she can barely say it, 'bastard, that monster again.'

I know it's wrong to let her go on thinking it was him who did me. But if I told her it wasn't him, she wouldn't be so sympathetic to me.

'That's OK,' I shrug. 'I have to . . . All those principles you and I share. I'm the only one who can get him . . .'

She looks at me with such tenderness. She touches my cheek and shakes her head as if she can hardly believe I am so brave, so full of dedication. She wipes tears away from her eyes then hisses between her teeth. 'We'll get that bastard. We'll get that goddamned bastard one of these days.'

She slips me into the paper angel wings saved from an old elementary school Christmas play. I flap my arms up and down like an angel and smile at her radiantly.

I wear a letter-sweater and loafers like a co-ed, a cheerleader's mini-skirt, a nurse's dress. I wear a pink conical hat and a satiny dress like a princess, the jeans and the pullover and ski-mask of a terrorist. I hold a fiercely triangular jacket with hefty padded shoulders that thins down to a minuscule waist.

'I can't believe the things we wore,' she giggles. She stands behind me, her hands on my shoulders as we look at my reflection in the mirror. She tucks my blouses in the back and smoothes my hair with her gloves.

When she tells me the message she breaks out of her usual dictation mode as if I really understand her now. She says, 'You tell that bastard this – you tell him I'll never – you tell him you'll never—'

He slouches on his throne. Behind us the great dining room is strewn with chewed breast and thigh and leg bones of fowl and game and dozens of empty bottles of wine and ale. We're alone. He pats the place beside him for me to sit. I squeeze in next to him. He puts his arm around me and says, sad and sentimental, 'I probably shouldn't tell you this. . . .'

But I want him to.

She removes her glasses and drops her face in her hands and sighs. The wrinkled sleeves of her shirt are rolled up, but her right cuff drags in a cold cup of coffee. The pencil falls from behind her ear and she doesn't pick it up. Her exhausted cabinet ministers retired hours ago for the night. I hear her kick her sensible shoes off under her desk. She rubs her temples. The dark bags under her eyes shift. She closes her eyes. 'I probably shouldn't admit this . . .'

But I want her to.

I almost asked about you then, dear Stan, but I didn't want to interrupt them. I know it was a lie for me to sit with them, to nod and murmur comforting-sounding nonsense syllables when I didn't mean them. I didn't do it because I was afraid of what they'd do to me if I didn't. I did it because I wanted them to owe me something. I wanted them to know that I knew something they wished they hadn't told. I wanted them to fear what I would do with the secrets that shamed them.

They start to ask about what they've forgotten. They want someone to say what's been denied.

Sometimes I try to sound academic, as if history were objective. I scratch my head and mention something almost casually, as if any school kid knows.

'Now what were the causes of the war?' 'Holy or civil?' 'Who fired the first shot?' 'What were the casualties?' 'How many lost?'

First one, dear Stan, then all of us.

For every war is a civil war, and every love denied is a double death.

I drop hints casually, in passing.

'Well, sure I'll tell him, but it'll have to wait until after he emerges from his Day of Abstinence Observation. Nobody, not even me, has access to him when he's fasting.'

'Fasting? *Him*?!'

'Sure. Everybody over there does now.'

'Well I'll be damned. . . .'

Or this:

'It'll be hard to get ahold of her then. She'll probably be out to lunch those three days, and not much good for a couple days afterwards. That's the May Day Down and Dirty Bash.'

'The what? *Her*?'

'Not just her – everybody. It's required.'

'Well, whadya know. . . .'

I say he actually abstains two days a week, and encourages wealthier citizens to follow his example in pledging the money he would have spent on food and drink to starving children. That she declares two glasses of hootch a day is medicinal. That he is considering a day-care centre for the Palace cleaning ladies' use. That she has lifted the ban on hunting for sport.

I know these things sound far-fetched, Stan, but some of them are almost true. And others will be, Stan, when you come back.

'That other kid?' His Highness asks, off-handedly, his mouth full of mutton.

'Yea?'

'You know, the other guy. I had you drop some stuff off for him in a park a while back?' He must be teasing me. Surely he knows how much I think about the boy.

'Yea.' I try to say coolly, 'What about him?'

His Majesty spits out a knot of gristle. 'Had to axe 'im.'

My eyes sting as I stare at His Highness. 'Oh?' I whisper.

He finishes chewing, swallows with a big gulping noise and chomps another hunk off the chop. 'He screwed up that pick-up. Grabbed the wrong bag. We can't afford those kinds of mistakes.'

A voice I barely recognize slips out of me. 'Right.'

He licks the grease off his lips then sighs. 'Yes ... I always hate having to nail little guys like that, but this one had it coming.'

I've got it coming too. I shudder expecting him to tell me it was my fault for dropping the wrong tape. 'How do you figure that?' I croak.

'Well, recently,' he sticks his pinkie far back in his mouth to dislodge something from a molar, 'I'd been getting wind of some pretty far-fetched sounding stuff. No way it could have been true.'

Obviously, he's enjoying prolonging my punishment. 'I see. . . .'

'But now we've off-ed the guy, we're in better shape. But this guy was only part of the problem, see?' He tears off another bite and talks with his mouth full. 'He couldn't have worked alone. There was a dame involved.'

'A dame?' I gulp.

'Call it a hunch, call it I've been around goddamn long enough to know that wherever there's trouble, there's always a dame.' He sprays me with grease when he shakes the chop to make his point. 'Take this whole ridiculous war itself. Never woulda happened except one dame gets uppity.'

I don't say anything until he looks up at me. 'Yessir.' I can't believe he doesn't suspect me.

'It's about time you learned this one. Unless you wanna end up like him. *Don't dink around with enemy girls.*'

'Yessir.' I lower my head, hoping he can't see that I'm blushing.

He stretches his arms out, hits his chest with his fist and burps loudly. 'What this unfortunate business with the other little guy has made clear, is that you need to work a little harder. We need to give you more training. You're a big girl now, eh little girl?'

'Absolutely, your Highness. Anything you say, sir.'

Both of them give me more to do. They make me drop things – packages I don't know the contents of – on the other side. I don't ask who picks them up.

I get overworked. But I can't complain to either of them without admitting that I spy for both, and that I also am conducting my own investigation into where you've gone, dear Stan, and trying to bring you back. I work so hard. I work all the time. I can't do everything. I stop my visits with the old folks at the border cottage.

I take refresher courses: how to quick change in a phone booth, how to fake accents, which park benches and garbage cans are best for the passage of anonymous-looking brown-paper packages. How to carry on genteel conversations over cocktails and finger food about Masterpieces of World Lit. When to catch the last bus out. How not to leave a trail. Or conversely, how to drop an empty pack of Camel filterless from my black-gloved hand and walk away slowly, but deliberately, so whoever might notice the strong, ominous shadow I cast, but not remember my tell-tale tennis shoes. How to eavesdrop.

I go to parties to eavesdrop incognito. Before I go I recite to myself, *Do not be seen or heard. Don't talk.* This makes even the most ordinary small talk dangerous, the most mundane cocktail-party chatter, a threat. When someone finds me at the hors d'oeuvres table piling up a little plate with cocktail sausages and curry dip and miniature cheese-and-onion quiches, and asks me, with a polite nod of her drink, 'And what do *you* do?' or corners me at the bar, 'What brings you here?' I freeze. I stammer something inaudible or fabricate a choke on my mouthful of canapé and hope whoever has cornered me will be embarrassed enough to excuse herself and go find someone else at whom to mingle. But if she doesn't, if she stands patiently waiting for me to compose myself, then lifts her eyebrow expectantly, and I have to say something, I lie. I tap my shades and whisper, 'I'm in the entertainment business.' Or tug at the lapels of my carefully worn coat, and chuckle under my breath, 'I'm royalty in disguise.'

These ludicrous postures are fun for a while. But only for that short while after I get the hang of the accents, the in-house names to drop, the false humility; and before my luck runs out. One of these days I am bound to introduce myself as a celebrated exile from the Eastern bloc to someone who is.

I'm afraid of being caught.

What if someone drags me from the party or chases me out into a busy street in a large South American city I don't know? What if they slap me in a dank cold room, force me to stare at a harsh overhead bulb hanging from a cracked ceiling? What if they insult me, or call me traitor or murderer or fratricide or uppity? What if they say I am a liar? What if they yank me by my hair and yell at me, their mouths and teeth and tongues against my face? What if they break my kneecaps

71

and kick me down on the floor and make me beg? What if they make me tell them?

I'm not allowed to use the phone. They say if I was, that in no time at all I'd be tying up the line chattering with all my little friends. They have no idea what I'd really use it for. They also say the lines could be bugged.

But sometimes I just want to pick up the phone and call the Palace or the Central Office and say, 'Gotta message here (reading) blah ... blah ... blah' and then go take a holiday in Rio. It takes too long to scurry back and forth; I work so hard at making up excuses.

Sometimes I try to see it:

I walk to the phone booth. Camera pans the back of my rumpled, rain-soaked trenchcoat, my soggy fedora. I close the door of the phone booth behind me in real time, then fast forward to them answering. They're both there. She answers and calls to him excitedly. I can see her call him. At the same time I can see me in the phone booth, like a split screen. Then I can see him too, in the garage, fiddling around with something at the end of a big orange electric cord. She says, 'Oh hon, we're just so glad to hear from you! Where are you?' She has a touch of a southern accent, soft and a little slow. The line is crackly enough to suggest I'm calling from some faraway exotic land, but clear enough so I can hear them talk. I hear the shuffle as she passes the phone to him. I look out the steamy windows of the phone booth at the rainy street in some place I don't know. Another me looks at them, eye level, as if I were looking in at them through a window of their house, as if I stood there less than twenty feet from them, while they speak to the me on the end of the long-distance phone. That me looks out at the grey-yellow rain to see small, gold-skinned, almost-naked people scurry through the narrow streets. 'Well gee, it's great to hear from you, hon.' His voice is the voice of a sweet, kind man who wears cardigans and house slippers and potters in the garage with things that aren't too big or dangerous. She presses her huggably plump body next to him, trying to keep her ear near the receiver to hear me. I can see the two of them as clearly as I see the two of me. I see her apron wrapped around her middle, her flour-coated hands, his checked flannel workshirt and his round, skinny, wire-framed glasses.

'I'm just starting the holiday baking for when you and Stan come back.'

He puts his arm around her, pulling her close so they can both listen as I tell them when I'm coming back.

72

What I imagine is as pretty, and as much a child's fiction, as a moon that's made of cheese, a flying carpet, what I imagine someday I will tell them.

It's been so long since I've stopped off to stay with the border guards, I worry that they, still under orders to let no one but me pass through, might not recognize me through my disguises and try to stop me. But they don't seem to notice that I've changed costumes. In fact, they don't seem to notice me at all. Even when I hunch across as a world series baseball team's equipment girl toting secrets in the hollowed shafts of a dozen baseball bats, even when I ask the two of them to help me carry the equipment (there is no team I'm travelling with), they don't notice me. When I'm a dowdy archeologist carrying micro-dots glazed into fake pre-Columbian pottery, or a baby with a message sewn into the lining of my diaper, they don't question me. They just keep dealing one another pairs.

Once, I'm a world-famous child ballerina, a monstrously precocious media darling who's made no secret of my desire to defect to the land of Coca-Cola and convertibles, I stop at the border house and tap my pretty, expensively manicured fingers on the kitchen window. They don't look up. I make a fist, rub a clean circle on the dirty surface hoping my tight-fitting, flesh-coloured tutu may grab the attention of at least one of them.

'Excuse me,' I announce prissily, 'Aren't you supposed to check my papers?'

Their game continues uninterrupted.

'Don't you know who I am?' I flash my jacket open and closed over my tight little bodice. One of them lays a hand down on the table with a gentle, but triumphant, smile.

'Don't you realize what I'm carrying?' I screech.

The glass gets misty with my breath. I bang my ballet slippers against the glass. Embedded in their thickly bound toes are electronic microdata sensor chips crammed full of earthshattering information.

One of the old guards at the table rubs her chin and squints, trying to figure out how her partner got such a winning hand so quickly. I drop my slippers and press my hands and face to the glass.

'Hey guys,' I whine, 'it's me . . .'

They don't look up.

The only clue His Highness gives is that you'd worked with a dame, Stan. And that rule: *Don't dink around.* So naturally, I do. With enemy girls. Every one I sleep with is an enemy.

I get the business over with, and then, pretending to sleep, wait until she sleeps. I can tell when she sleeps by the breath. When she is asleep, I lean up on my elbow and look. I watch the trembling of the soft-as-baby's eyelids I have, only moments previously, touched with my tongue. To test the degree of restfulness, I touch, very gently, with the tips of one, sometimes two, fingers, the perfect, tender, milk-coloured creases of the insides of the elbows. If she doesn't move, I lie as close as I can to her, while not allowing the skin of my body to touch the skin of her body.

Every sleeping person's skin feels, to the touch, precisely different – gritty or velvet or sandy or fine or oily as olive or cool. I never, ever, pretend to myself that the person whose skin I am touching is anyone other than who she is. However, while body temperatures do vary somewhat, some of them are similar enough so that if I close my eyes and lie not close enough to touch the skin, yet close enough to feel the temperature, I can pretend, sometimes, that the warmth that I sense next to me comes from someone who is not.

Until she breathes. I have no illusions about this either; the sound and movement of every person's sleeping breath is as distinctive as a face or fingerprint. But sometimes I put my face beside this girl's so I can hear her breathe more closely. I listen carefully because sometimes the pace of sleeping breath, along with the movement of the eyelids, reveals the content of the dreamer's dream. I listen to this breath and, if it's right, I listen to her pulse as well. And if I can tell that the content of her dream is what it needs to be, I lean to her and whisper, loud enough so she can hear, but soft enough so she will not awake. I ask about you, Stan. I watch the movement of her slightly parted lips, the line that opens to the dark inside of her, and hope she'll tell me.

Sometimes she murmurs or breathes deeply, her chest trembling as it rises and falls. But if she ever speaks, it's only to wake. She shakes her head like a fly is on her nose and swishes her arms. Her startled eyes open and she snaps, 'What are you doing?! What do you want?' not knowing I'd been watching her with true desire.

When she becomes upset by this, I pretend that I've been talking in my sleep. I murmur some foreign-sounding syllable and turn away. When I hear her fall back asleep, I leave; I always leave.

I didn't sleep at night, dear Stan; I looked for you. Already I was overworked by both of them. I worked too hard. I got too tired. I started to doze on the bus. Sometimes when I reported to them, I almost forget what I said.

After a while, I lost patience with that method of trying to find you.

I started rushing through the ol' one-two with these enemy girls. I came to regard the ol' one-two as an annoying preparation, a payment in advance for what would be a fruitless night of watching, asking, of not being answered.

I decided I needed a new approach.

I murmur things to this enemy girl when she's awake, some sweet nothing about how pretty are her sky-blue eyes and hands. She stops me.

'What?' I affect a sleepy innocence.

She sits up straight. She folds her white hands over her lap and shakes her head. 'You're not talking about me.'

I lean up on my elbow and say, in an overly halting voice. 'So – sorry – ees language prroblem.'

'No,' she says firmly, 'you meant what you said.'

'I – I guess I did.' I shrug, suddenly fluent. 'You've caught me.'

She stares at me. After we've been silent for so long I'm getting uncomfortable, I ask. 'Aren't you going to yell at me?'

'No.' She drops the end of this word like a knife; it sounds familiar.

I gulp, hoping I'm wrong about who I think she works for. 'Aren't you going to turn me in?'

Evenly, without raising her voice, without emphasizing one word over another, so generic and objective and passionless it has to be true, she says. 'You'll have to do that yourself.'

She nods to the clothes I've flung over the back of a chair. I slip from the bed which is the temperature of her. I get dressed in the cold and leave.

Why don't I just call them and turn myself in? Sometimes I almost see myself pick up the phone that I am not allowed to use, and call.

Late night. Camera pans the street to a skinny box of murky yellow light. Drops of rain catch the orange of the streetlights. I'm in the phone booth. This time I'm going to be direct. I'm going to tell them straight off who I am, dear Stan, and what I've done.

I pick up the receiver. I don't have to dial because someone picks it up immediately.

'Hello, it's me—' I start to say, but I can't tell them, because they're saying, 'We know, we're watching you.'

It won't be long now, Stan.

I realize that they send these girls to me. They do it to catch me.

They don't expect me to resist those strong square-jawed Olga's, those stern dark Natasha's, those pretty little soft-skinned Misha's. I know they bug the rooms I follow these girls to. That shaggy lampshade hides a camera, a mic to render permanent our brief interrogation. But I outwit them. I don't tell these girls anything important. The meaningless sweet nothings I pass on to them are in the public domain. Surely my bosses, more than anyone, remember that there is an extra layer of protection when consorting in a foreign language. I don't say anything that could be used against either of my governments or me. I'm not out to prove anything to these girls. No midnight tours of the embassy, no drinking of the state champagne, no bragging about the importance of my lone-ranger diplomacy to the cold war. I know my place. I know what a secret is for. In fact, I'd rather these girls didn't know what I did for a living. Though then, of course, they wouldn't be sent to me.

I decide to go for a direct approach, to say things to them which are not completely far-fetched fabrications; rather things which are similar to, if not exactly representative of, things I actually wonder, feel or need.

I run my index finger down the side of her neck and whisper very intimately. 'There's this guy . . .'

Her eyes are closed, but the way she shifts her shoulder, the way her pulse feels under my skin, lets me know she's listening. 'He's sort of . . . a lot . . .' I say this slowly, to make her wonder, prolong her anticipation . . . like me . . .' I barely nod to the chair I've flung my trenchcoat across. Though her eyes are closed, I know she senses my movement perfectly.

If she had ever been the perfect girl for this, the one I had imagined, she wouldn't have opened her eyes, she would have sighed and I'd have watched the word form on her barely moving mouth. But what she does, is sit up abruptly and look, with her not very pretty eyes, across the room.

'Oh yea . . .' she yawns, not covering her less than perfect teeth, 'that ridiculous coat and hat . . .'

She closes her eyes and lies back down again as if she's sleepy.

'That's right.' Much as I loathe the direct tit for tat, I have to encourage her.

Her lips smack as if she's about to wake up after a long night and start pouting. 'Medium height, medium build?' she smacks as she turns over on her side, wrapping her white arms around the pillow.

'Yea, that's right . . .' I look at her freckled shoulders.

'No distinguishing marks?' She rubs her eyes.

'Yea, that's him,' I say too enthusiastically.

She sighs like she is settling in for a nice little snooze.

'Well?' I wait until I can't hold myself. I grab her shoulder. 'What about him?'

She knocks my hand off her. 'I don't know him,' she snaps.

'What do you mean you don't know him? You just described him!'

'I don't know him,' she repeats clearly. She swings her legs out from the covers and stands up. The small of her back is perfectly flat and smooth.

I stare at her back, the soft bumps of her spine. Usually I'm the one to leave. I yank the covers up over my suddenly cold skin.

'I don't know him,' she enunciates clearly, as if explaining something to a child. 'None of us know him.'

She knows that I ask everyone I do this with, that in fact I only do it to ask about you, Stan.

'Then how did you know so much about what he looks like—' I start to whine, before I realize why she knows.

I fling the sheet off me, determined to leave before her. But when I've put my feet on the cold floor, she settles back in the bed. Of course she isn't going to leave; I always leave. I hurry into my clothes, pretending I'm not watching her out of the corner of my eye. When she pulls the covers up, I smell her skin again. She punches the pillows huffily, impatient for me to leave.

I stand outside the door a couple of minutes expecting to hear the click of her transmitter, then her report to one of them. I listen at the doors on either side of her room for the whirr of a video. When I go down to the lobby, I expect to be grappled from behind by a couple of hoods, but no one is hanging around to catch me. The doorboy says, as he opens the door for me, 'Good day.' There's no big black sedan waiting for me on the street. The path is clear. I leave.

I could have called them easily, dear Stan. I could have made an appointment, or I could have barged right in, no appointment necessary.

I could have marched up to either of them politely, but firmly, and cleared my throat. I could have tapped either of them on the shoulder and said. 'Excuse me.' Or, if I was so goddamned intent on a little drama, I could have poked them in the ribs and snarled, 'This is a stick-up, reach for the sky.' I could have turned them around to face me, pulled the stupid hat off my head and revealed my identity. Then slowly, with great finesse, perfect tension, turned my clenched hand over, and opened it to reveal, not a gun, but an empty blue-marked palm.

I could have emptied my pockets and said. 'Here, dammit. This is *yours*. You're responsible for all this, you silly bitch, you stupid asshole bastard. Now, take it back.' I could have thrown their papers and envelopes and memo-pads and checklists and cassettes and microdots and paper sacks at their feet and stomped on them with my tennis shoes. I could have hissed with such chill that they'd shiver, 'I – I – d-d-didn't ask for this.' I could have sneered, 'Every fucking thing you ever did in your shitty little life was asking for this.'

I could have yanked off my ratty hat and my stupid plastic Groucho Marx glasses and nose and moustache ensemble and stuck my naked face right up to theirs and said very slowly, with great righteousness and determination, 'No-Fucking-Thanks.' Then like a snotty adolescent, *'Don't tell. Don't hang around,'* and flipped them the bird. I could have stripped that ridiculous coat off my back, turned my bare ass on them, and walked out in my birthday suit.

But what is true is not told easily, and telling true does not undo what's done.

Does not break walls. Does not bring back what's lost. Does not make dead boys live.

I could have crumpled down in front of them and said I'm sorry.

I shuffle in, my eyes half-mast, and recite, in the chilly monotone of a sleep-walker, 'I'm bringing you a message from Her Honour . . .'

'Don't mumble fergodsake! Now what did you say?'

My eyes don't focus. I take a breath, 'I'm bringing you a message from Her Honour . . .' Then silent, fluid as a mime, I pull out the message I've written so carefully from her dictation. The envelope crackles when I remove the single sheet. My head drops. 'Sir . . . we are in receipt—'

'Stop!'

'Huh?' I sway.

'Stop, fuckwad!'

I sway to attention. My arms and legs feel heavy as they surface from sleep to waking.

'Open your goddamned eyes!'

I do, then close them again.

'That's my message to him, goddammit. Don't you know where you are?'

I look at her behind her wide oak desk. 'I got confused,' I whine, 'just for a second.'

'You're not in his goddamned pisshole of a Throne Room.' She knocks her in-basket over when she snatches my shoulders. 'You're here!'

'Yes ma'am.'

Her gloves grip me tight. 'I hope you don't do this often.'

'I don't,' I plead, oblivious to her sarcasm. 'I just got tired. I can't keep this up.'

'How do I know you won't fall asleep on the job at his place and drop some vital secret of mine?'

'I won't – it hasn't happened before—'

I don't think either of us believes me.

'Someone's double-crossed us.'

The voice is behind the bright white light in front of me. All I can see is white.

'Where am I?' I can barely hear my own voice.

Another voice from behind the light: 'Far-fetched fabrications.'

I try to shield my eyes with my hands. 'Is this where Stan—'

'We have convened this Tribunal to discover who is saying those terrible things.' The first voice interrupts me.

'There's a reason—' I blurt.

The voices are silent, waiting for me to convict myself further. When I blink, I see coloured spots. 'It wasn't me!'

'Additionally, secrets were leaked of an intimate nature. Things only someone in your position would know.'

More silence.

'I wasn't the only one privy to both sides—'

'You admit you're a double-crossing cunt! You're just like her!'

'I'm not.'

The other voice: 'You two-timing bastard! Just like him!'

'I'm not.'

I turn my face back and forth trying to face the faces I can't see.

'You two-faced—'

'No. I'm only one—'

'You can't deny—'

'I don't but—'

But I have, dear Stan, each thing I've done since you.

'If it wasn't you, who was it?'

I look up at the hot white lights. I can just barely see two dark shapes.

You must understand, dear Stan. I was there with them. I knew what they could do to someone in my position, someone alive and present and in the room with them, and littler than them. Anyone, Stan, even a baby, would do what I did to watch out for myself.

'Who was it?' they asked again.

I squinted at the light and saw, again, more clearly this time, two dark figures.

'It was him,' I said. 'It was that boy. He was wrong from the start.'

Dear Stan, you were. I wish you'd never come to see the two of them, and me, and what we'd drive ourselves to do.

'He shouldn't have been trusted from the start,' I gabbled on. 'He should've been watched.'

'You were supposed to watch him.'

'I did—'

'You did, and then?'

'I left.'

'He asked you not to leave.'

'It wasn't my fault—'

'You left.'

'You did too!' I screamed up at the shapes in the light. 'I was only doing what you did first. Why didn't you watch him? I didn't want him. He wasn't mine. He was yours. You left first.'

My face is smacked. Something I can't see in the brightness slaps my skin. I fall down. My face stings. Leather gloves. I touch the ground like a blind person. They don't say anything. I sit on my butt and pull my knees up to my chest.

I'm caught. No matter what terrible lie, what terrible truth I tell.

The light fades. I glance out of the corner of my eye to see the door. I wonder if I could out run a couple of middle-aged tyrants overburdened by their blood-soaked robes of state.

I trip over the soggy hem of my coat as I run out of the Throne Room, out of the Central Office, to the bottom of the long slim avenue of poplars, across the flagstone plaza to the border. Someone's shoes pound after me.

The loudspeakers in the squares of both cities, the radios, TVs, towncriers, shout the same message. I see it written, in the blur as I run, in the common-language newspaper they now share. I've brought them back together, Stan. The two of them are allies now against me.

I jump into the back of a van that is carrying, under the auspices of a new trade agreement, exotic foodstuffs and political manifestos across the border. I cower in a dark corner behind some crates. My body jerks as the truck rattles over roads undergoing expansion to accommodate the heavy trade traffic.

In the newly refurbished, expanded border house, two brisk young guards in ski-caps examine the van driver's papers. The two old border guards aren't anywhere I can see. The new guards speak haltingly in their newly common tongue. I close my eyes when I hear the back door of the van yanked open. Light spears through the cracks of the crates and cuts me. Two new young border guards leap on to the truck. They rip into sacks of nuts with their bayonets, knock the butts of their guns on a box of mangos, on barrels of apricot cider. They kick the crate I crouch behind and a few mandarin oranges roll on to the floor. One of the guards, a pretty boy whose unshaved face shines with excitement, jabs one of the oranges with his bayonet, then pokes it towards his partner. She laughs, snatches another in her petite black glove and heaves it at the boy. Missing the boy, it splatters against the wall of the truck like a snowball. They cover their mouths with their hands to stifle their laughter. They push each other off the truck and slam the door closed behind them. The air smells of citrus. The truck jolts to a start.

On another trip back, I have to stand in a long line at the slick new border-crossing complex. I look for the old border guards to wave me across, but they're gone. The new ones slowly examine the passports and contents of every suitcase carried by tourists, ambassadors, traders.

I realize who they're watching for.

While the efficient guards are making small talk with a group of students in their common tongue that I don't understand, I slip out of line. I backtrack to the entry to passport control, and exit through a side door. I can't go through that checkpoint anymore.

Instead, I try to get away from them by scrambling over treacherous mountain peaks their roads don't reach. I hack through a jungle with a rusty, almost bladeless tool I stole from a garden. I slither on my belly through an underground passage. I shut my eyes and dive in a fast-moving river. I flop, sputtering, my arms swishing on the white, white ground.

I think I see signs that someone's been here in the outlands before me, Stan. Footprints, the marks knees make when they fall in the dirt. I pray it's you, dear Stan, that even if you can't come back, I can leave them far enough behind so I can find you.

One dark cold night, there is a storm. As usual, I'm running away, trying not to be seen or heard or caught. Which is especially easy tonight. Everyone is inside. And even if they weren't, they wouldn't see me because it's everywhere, and everything, including me, is covered. Everything is white. It swirls around me. It falls from the sky. It pops from the ground and shoots from the horizon. It comes out of my skin and eyes and from my cold blue hands. It sounds like white noise, like my head against the pillow at night, or the noise between the pauses on a long-distance phone. There's nowhere to go, but I have to walk to keep from turning into it.

I see a pinprick of light in the gauze-coloured sky. I can't tell how close or far it is. I trudge towards it. As I get closer, it changes from a cold white pin to a warm yellow sphere. It's the glow of light in the window of the old border cottage before it was refurbished.

The white is getting higher around the tops of my basketball sneakers, up to my calves and knees. When I blink, flakes of it melt across my eyes. My coat is thin, I've lost my gloves, my hat is brimless and holey. The toes and soles of my tennis shoes are open. My legs are stiff unfeeling chunks. I lift them and pull them with my hands, as if my body was a doll's, towards the house.

I stumble to the window. I rub a circle in the frosty glass. Inside the room I see a tea kettle on the stove, ladles and spoons and pans on the hooks on the wall above the stove, a towel draped over the neck of the faucet by the sink. Bottles of home-jarred fruits are on a shelf. A cabinet of unmatched cups and plates. Sitting at the table playing cards, the two old guards. I see, like two exposures on one print of film, my white, freezing face upon the room. Flung over the back of the fourth chair of the table is a raincoat. Sitting at the third chair with his back to me, is someone else. He's playing cards with them.

I tap the stump of my frozen hand against the glass, but no one turns.

I see the toes of the kid's hi-tops hanging in the air beneath the table.

'Hey—' I start to call to them, but when I open my mouth, air frosts my lungs.

I sweep my arms up and down on the glass like a desperate game of angels in the snow. I try to sweep the white off but it keeps falling. I press my ungloved hands against the glass. My skin freezes, blue against the window.

Slowly, the boy at the table turns to watch me. I see his pretty face, his rose-coloured lips. He lowers his cards very slightly, but far enough so I can see the colour of his hands. The two old card players lower their cards too. All three put their cards down on the table. Then one, then both, all three of them, raise their uncovered hands and wave to me. I see the blue marks moving with their hands. The gesture they make says, 'Come back, come back.' I push the window but it won't move.

I'm going to walk around to the front door of the house. I want to go back in.

When I pull away from the window the frozen skin tears off my hands. I can't feel the house. I swish my arms in the falling air. I can't feel anything. I can't see the house. The white storm is surrounding me. I'm lost.

one. To accept of them, I didn't want that approval; I would not
have a stand-on-the-chair-type of thing with their minds. The
gesture they made says, "Come back, come back," when the chance
for it long passed.

I'm going to walk around to the back door of the house. I want to
back in.

Why it had sent from the window the image and that of an
understanding group. Stay? Try a time in essence to the village
and school I belonged, can't see the knows this my mind yet
surrounding me. I'm some

4

The Reign of Terror

Everybody went across the wall. I didn't want to. I wanted to storm it. I wanted to tear the border down. I said the other side was something different: the Prison.

I had a two-fold strategy. First, I recruited a party. I targeted my recruits carefully. I did not try to gather either those who could stand my height, or higher, or look at the horizon and see the wall for what it was, or look me in the eye and see similarly and tell me 'no'. Nor did I want the happy home-bodies. I wanted the ones who weren't easy, but were possible. I liked to spot the ones who wouldn't join just any group, but would, with the right persuasion, join me. I recruited from the nervous, the shifty, those with shady pasts, the secretive, the impressionable, the too-controlled, the curious, those looking for a change, the accidents begging to happen.

At first when I approached them and said what I said, they gawked, open-mouthed in exaggerated gestures of disblief. They shook their heads, 'That's impossible, unnatural'. I'd nod suggestively to the fuzzy border where earth meets sky, where the bus was huffing towards, and ask, in my evocatively hushed voice, 'Have you ever met anyone who's come back?' I dropped the end of my sentence like a knife. They'd slowly shake their heads. Then I'd step closer and whisper, 'Haven't you ever wondered what it's *really* like over there?' They'd gasp. Then I'd say words like 'commerce', 'trade', 'retirement' and 'compromise', with such loathing and disgust I frightened them. They'd widen their eyes, part their lips slightly, waiting for me to say more. But I held my ground silently, milking the fact that they wanted me to go on, but waiting until they did what they had tried not to do, what they had been told they'd perish if they did, what they had told themselves they would never want to do: they nodded yes.

I put my lips close to them and told them quietly, more quietly than the voice of reason had ever been, that beyond the harmless-looking horizon, on the other side of the border was – the Prison. Therein which were done things utter and unspeakable. Things which, if they, like everyone, toddled unthinkingly on to the bus, would happen also unto them. They'd gasp again. Then bite their pretty lower lips and shudder. Then lower their eyes, then slowly look up at me, then sadly shake their sorry heads, then lower their faces on to my shoulder and sob. Thus they succumbed.

I let them sniff on my shoulder for a bit. Then I lifted their pretty faces, knowing that they'd be seeing me through teary eyes like a movie shot through a gauze filter. And I'd say, my voice evocatively hushed, that all was not lost. That they could join the Party. That they could do a Great Thing with the wreck (I'd made) of their shabby little lives. That they could join the crusade.

I made them memorize the party line I'd written. I printed up a bunch of manifestos. I made them memorize the party line I'd written. Before there was actually a party I said that there was because I knew the importance of numbers. The truth I told these pretty, impression-able recruits depended on my mood and on their particular suscepti-bility. I told some of them I was merely revising the true original way we all were meant to be before the terrible war, before the ugly building of the Prison. I told others they were select, the chosen few, determined by their marks to be crusaders. Others that this was a great opportunity, that the world was changing and when the changes had occurred they would be on top. I tossed around words like 'mission', 'truth', 'honesty', like they were going out of style. I told them I'd found what was lost. I said the principles. I let them carry the flag. I made promises. Everybody loves promises.

The motto I taught was simple: *Don't*. And, like any call to arms, was simple to the point of being meaningless. I could just as easily, just as senselessly, have taught them, *Do*. As long as I spoke in absolutes, in impossibilities, I could tell them, and have them pass along to everyone, anything that helped me to my purpose, i.e. any damn thing I felt like.

Necessarily, the motto had variations. Explications made up and dragged out like overly jewelled, and consequently useless, ceremonial armour, whenever any of them, with my permission, felt like indulging a little more than usual. Such as: *Don't ever. No way. I didn't.* Such as: *It wasn't me.* Such as: *Someday what I will tell.* Or: *Not on your life.* Or: *Wild horses couldn't drag it out of me.* (Was there a hint of curiosity, a note of desire in this one? i.e. how exciting, how flattering to be dragged kicking and screaming, and what a vacation to be overpowered and therefore rid of the work – we all worked very hard, remember. And not only that, but what a memorable picture it might make? But I tolerated no such fantasies: they knew this.) Other variations of the motto: *It's defeat. It's cowardice. It's kissing goodbye to the principles.* Ours was a world of principles.

Principles expoused, or rather ranted, from the soapboxes and orange crates I mounted in market squares and flagstone plazas, and in the pamphlets I wrote and arranged the dispersal thereof. I stationed my charges at grocery stores and camp sites and outside banks and movie theatres and in public parks. I worked on my delivery. I rode around on the tops of carts and vans and yelled through a scratchy-sounding loudspeaker at tired commuters during rush hour. I screamed. 'It isn't destiny!' I yelled that they could, as easily as they could turn the tide, turn the tide. I shouted about strength and will and staying in shape and incorruptibility and watching out, not realizing as I yelled, because I yelled, my vocal cords were wearing down.

I outfitted my party in uniforms. I sent them to Goodwill with a tiny allowance and told them to get anything. I let them think they could each come up with their own independent fashion statements about rebellion and freedom, but I knew exactly what they'd look like. I had a bunch of private little graduation ceremonies. I stood them up and pulled their clothes on for them, buttoned and zipped and tied them. Always the same: baggie fatigues, hi-tops, inside-out sweat-shirts, uneven short-cropped hair, denim jackets with lots of pockets for pens and petitions and pamphlets, and on the breasts of which they wore an array or brightly coloured buttons emblazoned with the party motto, *Don't*.

But my strategy was two-fold. In addition to the band of committed young idealists, I presided over a covert inner circle of single-minded, no-nonsense extremists. The existence of which, the band, with their tail-wagging belief in telling the previously untellable, in getting secrets out into the open, had no idea. My inner circle met clandestinely, usually late at night, though sometimes we managed quickies on our lunch breaks. Twice we managed weekends away under the pretext that we were going away on business. We always met in places where we'd never been seen, or heard, again. We called each other code names from a code so secret none of us could, and yet so ingrained none of us needed to, decipher it. Names like 'Binkie' and 'Pookie' and 'Misha'. When we did meet in the light of day, we wore seamless stockings over our faces to press our features flat beyond recognition. We vowed, if ever any of us were discovered, to deny that there were more of us. And we carried about our persons individually cellophane-wrapped capsules that would enable each of us to do away with ourselves and the knowledge of our secret inner circle.

We did all this as I had taught. Because we knew, as also I had taught, that the party line about gradual turnings of gradual tides, about integrity and truth and lies, about the principles, was rigmarole. We knew – I taught – that real change, true and severing, occurs with blood, and only so, that is: with terror. I was a terrorist.

My secret, more direct agenda: to sabatoge the bus. To blow the border wall off the map. To storm the Prison. To bring back the bones.

I planned a day of distraction, a Sunday, the best day for these kinds of things. The committed young idealists marched through town behind their cute dawn-coloured flag. They wore their one-rebellion-fits-all uniforms and carried placards I'd recycled from a previous crusade. They shouted the silly motto and chanted the party line to the rhythm of a popular dance tune.

It was a beautiful Sunday afternoon; I couldn't have done better if I'd made the day myself. So everyone in town, almost, turned out to see it. Everyone simply wanted to get outside and enjoy the warm air and stand in the sun and bump into their neighbours and go eat fried chicken in the park afterwards. Some of the old dears from the brownstones, when they heard the commotion on the street, assumed it was a parade and grabbed their hankies and tottered downstairs to stand on the sidewalk and cheer the parade along. Only to find that it wasn't a parade, but a serious protest march. The poor dears let their hankies droop and let their toothless smiles sag and looked around with sad, puzzled looks. Then wheezed back upstairs and closed their windows. The crowds who stayed on the sidewalk on Main Street shook their heads and furrowed their brows and wrung their hands with concern for the future of these poor misguided young people.

The band ended their march with a rally on the front steps of the Court House. The press was there, skinny nurdy guys with wire-rimmed glasses and spiral notebooks, and good-looking girls with long blonde hair and suits and mikes in front of cameras. The tense, confused beardless police force hovered around hoping they wouldn't have to do anything. Some of the more agile youngsters leapt – the dear kids only ever acted with excess – up on to the stage I'd had set up for them. (Bless their hearts, they never thought of the practical things.) They waved their little purple banners in fluttery arcs while they sincerely, passionately, rudely, and with no idea, no idea whatsoever of their heritage, spouted words I had taught them but that they couldn't quite pronounce. They tried to sound as tough as they could, which wasn't very tough, given their high-pitched voices, when they shouted, 'This is war.' As if it was a civil – no – a holy thing. They went on and on and on about the principles and change and revolution and recovery and going back, etc. for hours. They didn't change anybody's mind.

Nonetheless, the rally served its purpose. I, of course, was not present at the widely publicized gathering, having told my dear young party, in my evocatively hushed voice, that I would be 'in danger'.

They thrilled when I spoke of the noble sacrifice a revolutionary might be forced, and should be willing, to make for such glorious principles. And they agreed, when I suggested carefully, in such a way as to make them think they had suggested it, that the principles would best be served in the long run by my absence from this particular event. So the rally, which I watched from where I was with my field glasses, did serve its purpose. Which was simply to distract.

For while they were causing such attention-getting hullabaloo downtown, the inner circle of extremists and myself had hidden ourselves in the poor part of town, past the park. We were hidden behind orange crates and in carts and in vans with busted out windows. Our fingers were poised on the triggers of our guns. Our noses were squished under the stockings we'd pulled over our faces. We sweated beneath our skin caps. We could faintly hear, from not far off, the happy chirps and squeaks of animals in the zoo. We held our breath and listened. We were waiting for the bus.

Which would come, as it always, always did. Though the march route I'd planned might throw the bus off route or delay it, it would come. The street by the bus stop was empty. Everyone who could, except my inner circle and myself, had gone off to see the march. And everyone who couldn't was a passenger. But we couldn't predict, despite our studies and intelligence, and we couldn't sense, despite our sharper eyes and ears, and I couldn't tell, despite my field glasses, exactly when the bus was coming. But the old folks knew, before we did, when the bus was on its way. We saw them timidly open the front doors of their run-down homes, then step gingerly down their sagging steps, then stumble along on their walkers and canes, their shaking hands on one another's arms. They wore their Sunday dresses and suits and sensible shoes and hats. They carried, or pulled along on little shopping carts, their scuffed up overnight bags. They lined up at the rickety bus shelter, a thin little roof with a glass back and three open sides. They stood there patiently. The gents, who were far outnumbered by the ladies, tipped their tweedy hats to the gals or offered them their arms. The ladies wore gloves and little box hats, a few of them with light mesh veils.

My inner circle watched them through squinted eyes, through the muddy beige of their face stockings. They couldn't see much. But I watched through the cold sharp lens of my field glasses, and I saw close-up, an uninvited intimate, their toothless chewing cheeks, their trembling chins, their croaked hellos and trembling nods, the smiles they traded sweetly with each other. I saw their watery eyes, and how they craned their eager, hopeful necks first east, from whence the bus would come, then west, towards the horizon-wall – the Prison. Only I, among my followers, saw the movement of the old folks' lips when they said the name of the place we couldn't see.

'To Prison,' I hissed beneath my breath. Then listened to the rustle of my circle repeating after me, 'To Prison, to Prison'.

When I saw, though I didn't let my inner circle see, the old folks' faces brighten, when I saw them clutch each other's arms, then wave, I knew the bus was coming. The old bus lumbered up the sleepy street like a buffalo. The hood of the bus was fat and round. The semi-circles of chrome above the bright, shiny glass of the headlights looked like eyebrows raised in cheerful surprise. Between the headlights, the giant grill smiled like a friendly, dopey human-faced truck. The bus had dark sunscreen windows along both sides. The bus creaked towards the bus stop then sputtered to a halt. The old folks started to pick up their baggage. My circle whined as eager as puppies behind me. I glared back at them to wait.

The bus stopped. The old folks waited for the door of the bus to open. The door unfolded slowly with a squeak. The old folks politely said, 'After you,' 'No, after you,' 'No after you,' to each other as they all got on the bus. I saw them hold their fellow's elbows, or put their hands gently on the small of their neighbours' backs to help them mount the steps. It took them ages to get on the bus. I drummed the fingers of my black-gloved hand on the case of my field glasses. Behind me, my inner circle tapped their fingers on the triggers of their rifles and moaned like dogs; I shushed them.

I could see, through the dark windows of the bus, one or two of the less fragile old gents take it upon themselves to hoist all the overnight bags on to the racks above the seats. I could see, through my binoculars, the silvery lines of their trembling arms moving up and down in the aisle. When they were all settled in their seats, the door slowly folded shut. The bus coughed a couple of grey clouds of exhaust and lurched forward. I saw, through my binoculars, through the black tint of the bus windows, their wrinkled faces facing each other and smiling their crinkly smiles. I saw their old mouths open. I waited until I could see the rows of their white heads swaying back and forth in the rhythm of their holiday song. As the last little ray of sunshine shot down on me, I saw, in a flash, myself reflected in the dark windows of the bus.

I flung my black-gloved hand into the air and snapped my fingers. My inner circle snapped to attention. I chopped my hand down, and my followers and I poured into the street like rats. I squatted in front of the oncoming bus in my sharpshooter stance, aimed my rifle at the driver's window, and yelled, 'Stop!' The veins popped out on my neck. 'Get off the bus or I'll shoot!' The bald tyres of the bus squeaked to a halt. Though I demanded their obedience to me, I was pissed off that they surrendered so easily. Why didn't the bastard behind the wheel try to run me down? I heard the feeble cough of the dying motor and the sad, puzzled silence after the folks stopped singing. Then a couple of pitiful cries from inside. 'What is it? Who is it?'

'Shut up and get off the goddamned bus!' I screeched. I tromped up to the front of the bus and smashed my rifle through the driver's window. Glass shattered everywhere.

'You doddering old fucks aren't going anywhere!' I growled as I pressed my body against the hot steamy grill of the bus. I pushed the end of my rifle into the face of the driver I didn't bother looking at. I felt his neck shift when he gulped beneath the chilly metal. 'Off the bus!' I screamed. Nobody moved. 'Off the goddamn bus! And bring your jackass little overnight bags with you! Now move! Out!' I spat through the sticky beige stocking over my face. My circle stood around the bus door. It opened with a shy, scared squeak. Slowly, timidly the frightened seniors stumbled off the bus. One of my toughs yanked the luggage from them, and another shoved them into a line in the rain. It was raining now, suddenly overcast and cold. I ordered a couple of my hoodlums to go through the luggage. I was looking for the secret message they carried. My charges kicked the cases open. They jabbed their bayonets looking for hidden pockets or concealed panels. But what they found: flannel nighties, sensible shoes, support socks, old dop kits with initials tooled into the leather, extra pairs of glasses, soft-edged photographs of kids and grandkids, lockets with portraits, packets of letters in string. In other words, nothing I valued.

The old folks were standing single file, their weak old arms raised towards the soggy skies.

'On your knees, geezers! Down!' They fell into the mud. 'Now, flat on your bellies. Then nobody makes a move!' They wheezed and flopped down until their faces were in the mud. I walked behind them and yelled at their trembling backs. 'Now listen, you old fucks, and listen up good!' I spun around when I saw, out of the corner of my eye, one of them move. An old man was turning his hearing aid up. I chuckled.

'I'm here to rescue you,' I announced.

None of them moved. I realized I had planned this wrong. What I would have liked, upon their hearing the announcement of the freedom I was offering them, would have been for them to have bent down on their knees to me. But they couldn't as I'd already forced them to their bellies. 'Now get grateful or else!' I stamped my foot for emphasis, splattering mud on the tweed jackets of two old guys nearest me. I cleared my throat. 'I said, I'm here to *rescue* you.' No response. 'Don't you stupid old fucks realize where that broken down meat-mobile is taking you?!' I screeched.

Still, no response. 'Goddammit, I'm rescuing you!'

My followers watched me watch the cold, wet old folks shiver in the mud. My toughs behind me shifted back and forth from one squeaky tennie to the other. We listened to the dull, even sound of the rain. I heard a sniff, then a voice behind me, sputtering into the mud, addressing me, 'But we don't need to be rescued.'

I spun around to see who was talking to me. A little old lady, probably all of five feet tall, if I ever let her stand up again. Her lips were moving against the veil the mud pressed to her face. 'Except from you.'

I stamped over and yelled down at the soggy coat on her back. 'Don't tell me what you need, granny. I know what you need!'

She didn't move.

Then I heard another creaky voice further along the line. 'We don't need to be rescued—' I spun back around and I heard an old guy gulp, 'except from you'. I tromped over and raised my hi-top above his frosty head, then heard another voice, quick and quivery, back near the first lady. 'We don't need to be rescued—' I stepped towards her then heard another voice further down the line complete her sentence, 'except from you'. Then the first old gal started up again, 'We don't need to be rescued—' I whirled back to face her. A lot of them were saying it, not all at once, they never interrupted each other, but they helped each other finish the sentence few of them seemed strong enough to say alone. I kept turning back and forth from voice to voice. They all were telling me, 'We don't need to be rescued, except from you.'

I took a few steps back from the line of them and looked at their filthy soggy coats and shoes and hair. I looked around at my impatient inner circle. They stood as I'd taught them to, legs spread shoulder's width, ready to strike, faces covered by stockings and dark ski-caps, fingers twitching on the triggers of their guns. We didn't look like rescuers.

Didn't the old folks know where they were going? Did they expect me to believe them just because they did?

When I said quietly, to no one in particular, 'But this is a rescue mission,' no one challenged me.

I watched them lay there a long, long time.

Then something happened. One of them lifted his mud-spattered face from the ground and said, in his thin old man voice, 'I won't leave.'

I marched over to where he shivered on the ground. I squatted down to look at him. He had milky eyes with faded blue irises and yellow skin on his eyelids. His tear ducts were red. There were lines of red, thin as hair, on the grey-white whites of his eyes. His pale lips barely moved. 'I'll stay instead.'

I didn't want my skin to flush, but it did, with the old thrill of my recruiting days when they'd succumb. But I stopped myself. I shook my head and stood up abruptly. I didn't want that. The kids were watching me from behind. They'd stepped closer a step or two. Their eyes were shifting beneath the stockings over their faces. They wanted some action. They wanted some action now.

I looked down at the old man's body, skinny as a stick. My crew tapped their fingers restlessly on their triggers. I looked back down at the old man, then the whole line of old people. There were a lot of them, a whole busload of them. There would be another busload after this one. Then another. They were all alike. The loss of any one of them wouldn't make anything different.

I looked away, flung my gloved fist into the air, and snapped my fingers. My right-hand girl and right-hand boy panted up behind me. I could smell the healthy fresh smell of the sweat of my right-hand girl. I turned to her. Underneath the stocking on her face, her red mouth glistened. Her perfect white teeth smiled at me. I looked at her mouth then gave a sharp nod of my head down at the old man. She made a noise like laughter in the bottom of her throat then slapped me on the back. I felt the hot sting of her hand on my back. It was the only time any of us had touched each other like that without something else. I spun around on my heels and walked away. I wanted her to watch me walk away.

Then my two right-hand kids hoisted the old man up from the mud by his armpits. I watched the girl bend. Her back was beautiful. The old man didn't resist: he was loose as a doll. His modest Sunday suit was awry and one of his Hush-Puppies had slipped off his feet. The pair from my circle stripped him down to his sagging old-man underwear. He crossed his arms over his chest as if he could hide himself. The hair on his head was white and pale. His grey skin shivered. They slapped his arms up in the air and shoved an inside-out sweatshirt over his head. His skinny spotted hands stuck out of the rolled-up sleeves. They yanked a pair of baggie trousers up over his legs. The trousers hung on him. They pushed his feet into a pair of hi-tops. They forced a stocking over his face, pressing his startled features flat. They covered his pale head with a ski-cap. The guy shoved a cane into one of his hands, the girl thrust a rifle into the other. Her shoulders, when she forced him, were very smooth. The old man could barely support his burden. The two toughs kicked his feet apart, shoulder width, so he looked like he was almost ready to strike, but his arthritic knees were shaking. He couldn't balance the cane and the gun.

I looked at the shaking backs of the old folks weeping face-down in the mud. I looked at the grinning, eager faces of the kids I had recruited, then back at the pathetic crossbreed I'd created. He buckled under the weight of what I'd made him bear. He dropped the rifle, then dropped the cane, and then his body fell. I heard his body fall, a crack. Some of the old folks started to move, but I stomped my foot. I couldn't yell a command, but they knew to be still. The old man moaned some syllables I didn't understand. He swished his arms in the mud like a child playing angels in the snow, first quick and frantic, then slower. I stood above him and watched and didn't stop it. When I heard his rasp, I leaned down over him. I squatted, not kneeling, and lowered my ear close enough to see his pale lips move and to hear the slick sounds of the movements of his tongue and lips. He was trying to tell me something but I didn't hear. He wanted me to lean closer, but I didn't.

I stood up in the rain. I poked him with my rifle. He didn't move. I heard my right-hand girl walk up behind me. I smelled her skin behind me. 'Don't,' I said. 'Leave him.' I didn't want anyone, especially her, to see him.

I shouldered my rifle and stepped back to the line of old people. They lay patiently in the rain. I leaned down and snatched one up, roughly. But when I felt his thin arm on my glove, I loosened my grip and held his elbow gently. I took a breath and closed my eyes. When I opened my eyes I didn't look at him, but I tried to help him up gently. He sat up on his knees. His monogrammed jacket was smeared with filth. I wiped the mud from his face and his fine white hair with my glove. I gathered him by his armpits and helped him stand. Some of my followers, though not my right-hand girl, went to the other folks and helped them up. We cupped our hands beneath their trembling elbows and walked them to the bus.

I held the old folks' elbows as they slowly mounted the steps to the bus. I didn't step on to the bus, but I stood outside and heard them slowly shuffle to their seats. I heard them try to comfort one another. I looked away from the dark reflecting windows.

My right-hand girl stood beside me. This was the only time any of them spoke to me before I spoke to them. She jerked her head towards the crumpled heap of old man who wore our clothes. 'What do we do with that?'

I dropped my rifle and took off my gloves and dropped them. I dropped my face into my hands. My head, my coloured hands, my shoulders shook.

Everyone in my inner circle looked at me. I watched the still, unmoving heap that I'd made crumble. I fell down. The circle around me shifted. They hovered around me restless for a command. I heard them tap their fingers on the triggers of their guns. The rain increased. It was a storm. I couldn't hear what they were saying beneath the storm.

One of my followers walked up to me from behind. He snatched me up by my armpits and spun me around to look at him. I couldn't see much beneath the stocking that covered his face, except that he was grinning. He tapped my shoulder with the tip of his rifle like he was playing with me. 'What do we do with *this*?' he asked.

My right-hand girl stepped out of the circle. She walked up to me and this guy. She ran a smooth finger of hers down the strap of the field glasses I wore around my neck. She lifted the field glasses up over my head. She held the end of the strap and swung the glasses around in a fast dark circle in the air. We all looked at the circle like we were hypnotized. Suddenly she stopped spinning them and put them on over her neck. She stepped up close to me and put her mouth near my ear and said, as if she was saying it to the guy who'd asked, but loud enough so all the followers could hear, 'Don't'.

The guy who tapped me on the shoulder shrugged and slid back into his place in the circle. My right-hand girl leaned down and picked up my gloves. She held the palms of the gloves in her hand so the fingers of the gloves hung loose. When she smiled I could see her lips pressed white beneath her stockinged face. Then suddenly, before I could move, she'd slapped me on the butt with the gloves. She laughed. Everyone laughed.

She put the fingers of her left hand into the left glove and pulled the glove down at her wrist. She did the same with her right hand. She spread her fingers wide then meshed her hands together. She told her followers, in a voice too much like mine, 'Leave her'.

The circle split as quickly as if I had snapped my fingers at them. They followed the black-gloved girl with high steps.

Part of me wanted to wipe the mud from my knees and stumble after them, but I knew I couldn't keep up with them anymore. I also

97

knew that no matter how far I got from this spot, I would look back. And even if I got away, I would remember him, the still unmoving heap that I'd watched crumble.

I fell back on the ground. I heard the click then a whirr then a choke. The bus was starting. I saw little hiccups of black smoke come out of the back of the bus then the continuous trail of exhaust. I didn't know what the bus was waiting for.

I could just make out the shapes of the old folks' heads inside the glass. Everyone was settled.

I looked back at the black-gloved girl and her circle as they moved away from me. They frisked along like eager adolescents hitting each other on their upper arms and sparring with invisible targets in the air. They shouted dirty words and laughed loudly. The girl with the gloves threw her arm around the back of one of them and kept it there.

I worried that if the bus waited too long, the kids would come back and stop it, really stop it.

I stood up. My legs were stiff. I walked towards the bus. My body shook. I stood by the door of the bus and looked at the black corrugated hard rubber steps and the soggy, wet, chocolate-coloured track of mud that went into the bus. I looked at the dull metal pole at the base of the driver's seat.

Then someone's hand reached out to me. Someone took my naked hand and helped me on to the bus.

Whether in shame or sadness or in fear or something else I didn't know, I kept my head lowered. I pulled my rain-soaked ski-cap down further over my face. I let myself be led by this hand which belonged to somone I didn't look at. While this hand led me down the aisle of the bus, I also felt, beneath my elbows, on either side of me, the old folks' hands, supporting me. I felt their soft, weak, trembling hands help me along. Then someone's hand, the hand that I was following, patted the headrest of an aisle seat near the middle of the bus. It was the only empty seat on the bus. I put my shaking hands on the armrests and sat down slowly. My body creaked. I leaned back, exhausted, against the seat and closed my eyes. I felt someone's hand put a pillow behind my head and tuck a blanket around my knees. After a few seconds, I felt someone go away.

Everyone had come in from the storm and the heater was on so the bus was steamy and damp. I opened my eyes when I felt someone tap my arm. An old man was leaning across the aisle to me. He said, with utmost politeness, 'Your cap, my dear.'

He put his age-spotted hand out. I took my ski-cap off and handed it to him. He stood up and put it on the overhead luggage rack above me. He smiled at me, then kept on smiling longer than he needed to. The engine of the bus hummed. I kept looking at the man. I raised my neck and I took a hold of the bottom of the stocking that covered my face. I held it a second. I felt the little knots of nylon with the pads of my fingers. I pulled the stocking off. It was like peeling off skin. I felt the pattern of the mesh the hose had made against my skin. My features spread out, relaxing into shapes I had forgotten. I felt cool air against my face.

I handed the limp stocking to the man. He tossed it in the rack above the seat. His old arms stretched above me. When he'd put the things on the rack the way he wanted them, he looked at me again, this time, seriously, without a smile. He hesitated a moment, shrugged, then reached his smooth-skinned hand to me and touched me. His fingers smoothed my matted hair. I felt the cool, round tips of his fingers in my hair. When he took his hand away, he looked at me with his head cocked a couple inches like a hairdresser examining a cut. He looked at my face again and smiled. He patted me on the arm and sat back down in the seat across from me. Before he settled in, he stuck his hand into the inside of his jacket and pulled out a piece of paper and handed it to me – the songsheet. He wiggled back into his seat and placed his hands neatly on his knees. He tapped his fingers on his knees a couple of times. He looked back at me and smiled. Then he looked straight ahead and cleared his throat. He waited a couple of seconds before he leaned into the aisle and waved up towards the front of the bus. When he settled back in his seat, the bus started moving.

The inside of my body shifted when the bus moved.

It was too dark on the bus for me to see the words of the holiday songs. The folks didn't seem to need them. The folks had the words memorized, as if they'd prepared for this trip for a long time.

The darkness on the bus was from the sunscreen windows. But there was a spill of yellow-grey light from the front of the bus where I'd smashed the driver's window. I leaned into the aisle the way the old man across from me had done and looked up and down the bus. The bus was entirely full. I had been given the only empty seat on the bus. I looked up at the front of the bus. I could see the driver's hand on the wheel and, through the frosted glass panel dividing the driver's seat from the main part of the bus, an outline of the driver surrounded by light.

After we were underway, I leaned over the old woman who was asleep in the window seat next to me and looked outside. It was still raining, though much less now, and a dirty yellow light hung on everything. I could just barely see, because I knew where my former followers were hiding, the edges of their black ski-caps. I saw, following us as we moved, watching us, the binoculars. The tips of the rifles were aimed at us.

5

The Children's Crusade

I work so hard, I work so hard. I try to do things right, but it's so hard. I work and work and I think, oh god, it's not going to happen, and I almost give up. But then a little ray of sunshine breaks through the clouds, teasing me on the back of my neck, and I pick myself up off the ground. I'm out in the garden. I'm kneeling in the dirt. My dirty face is in my hands. I've been working and working, pretending I can, but knowing I can't, work hard enough and water and turn and dig and bury enough. But then, when I feel that little ray of sunshine on the back of my neck, I put my hand in my pocket. I put my fingers around the cloth. I lean back on my heels, I lift my dirty wet-stained face, my scratched hands to the heavens, and I thank them for a little ray of sunshine.

Then I get off my butt and dig frantically. I've been through all this before.

I yank dandelion and clover and nettles and crabgrass as fast as I can. I chop with my kitchen spoon. I fling everything in the air trying to look like a fierce and careless and indiscriminate machine. But I can't. It's only me. It's only a tiny spoon.

I wait for little rays of sunshine. I try not to. I try to be surprised by them, to receive them joyfully as grace, as icing on the cake, but I need them. But maybe I'm just being greedy. Maybe I'm just fat and decadent, addicted to icing on the cake when most of the world is starving. But I'm not. I'm thin, and that's why I started this garden anyway, to do my part. But I feel so terrible. I must be terrible. I try not to want but I do.

But it's not all I do is wait for little rays of sun. I work hard. I turn dirt, rearrange pebbles, pick at stones, dig a hole, cover things. I check my pockets. I'm putting up a trellis. Which, granted, is a stupid thing to do.

I find things when I'm picking around. Old pieces of broken glass, cement, the spoke of a wheel, a clip, a tape. I sort through them, save the dirt I crumble off and toss them aside. Not away. I haven't made a wall to throw what I don't need beyond. To each its own.

You wouldn't recognize the place, dear. It's so green and fertile. I've got dahlias and carrots and geraniums and magnolias and corn and peas. I've got some lovely dogwood and cherry trees. They'll be gorgeous in the spring, all those pink-white blooms as soft as skin. Potatoes, of course. Cabbages, both plain and festive. African violets. The violets are very difficult but you wouldn't believe what I can do now. I'm a regular green thumb! Why, you couldn't pick me out of a crowd of regulars! Even you! Why don't you come back in the spring? Just for a visit? When the blossoms are out and the cherry trees are in bloom?

I work very hard. Neither rain nor snow, nor dark of night or day. Nor sun, I suppose, though I haven't had many opportunities to enjoy the latter. Nor anything, really, could keep me from it. Except them, of course.

I don't mean to sound unpleasant about the rain. It isn't that bad. In fact I adore it. I adore lifting my face to it. I adore sloshing around in it like a kid in the sprinkler – no – I didn't mean to put it that way – I meant like a happy little duck in a pond. Then I come back inside – the place is great now, quiet and calm and clean – for a nice hot bath and a nice hot cup of tea. And I like watching the plants lift their sweet little faces to the rain. In fact, nowadays when I see those dark clouds I don't think, oh god, it's not going to happen, it's going to rain, nowadays I think, how terrific for the plants. I've changed. I think of silver linings now. But despite my newfound cheerfulness – have I convinced you? – about rain, I do wait for those little rays of sunshine.

I wish you would come back and smell the flowers, and listen to the crisp industrious click of my trusty spoon scratching away at the rock. We'll be safe here now. It's been so long and I've been so quiet and there's so little left to trample, Stan.

Surely this garden was always here, beneath, at least potentially, but we just couldn't see it. Maybe it had to be bashed open for us to see. Maybe they were only trying, in their overenthusiastic way, to help.

I remember your face in the morning after that night. I knew what the noise was the second I jolted awake; you didn't. You didn't want to. There was a whup of a sudden billow of cloth, and then the crack of the splitting of wood. Then all the noise. You buried your head in my shoulder. I held you for a moment while the windows, the walls, the bed of our cottage on the border shook apart. Then I leapt up and ran out back. They were there with their flashlights and their electric saw and dart guns and jackhammers and cart. Their tough little arms shook as they hammered. Their nasty leers, their perfect teeth, showed beneath the safety goggles they wore. We couldn't see their eyes clearly, but we could see the way they held their wrists, their shoes, enough to recognize them. You stumbled out a few seconds after me, crying. Oh, Stan, your beautiful weeping face was sad and shocked. You didn't see everything. You didn't see the dawn-coloured colours fall. But when you saw what you did, and you admitted it, you said you didn't want to see anything like that again.

I've kept your things where you left them so that when you come back you'll be able to find your way. Come back, dear Stan; they won't come back. Each day I am more confident. Each sprig of green, though pale and limp, each thin stick of the trellis, helps convince me.

I didn't go out for a long time afterwards. Long after you'd gone, long after I could follow the track you must have left, and find you. Long after their high-pitched voices left. I stayed as quiet as I could inside. Then, I went out very cautiously. It was a mess, a terrible wreck. Huge busted blocks of concrete, broken glass, bent red-streaked hunks of metal, dust covering everything like dirty sheets, so much to fall and be caught on. But I climbed carefully and looked. I squinted in a crack, and underneath, far underneath, much further than I could see, I could barely make out a tangle of colour. I pushed some cement chunks apart and dropped into the crack. I picked through dead brown branches, dry grey mulch that must have been there before us. I bumped into stuff with my tennis shoes. I found abandoned tools. They looked like they'd been dropped suddenly; a candy wrapper, a single arm off a sprinkler, a pole, a rag, a mop and pail. Someone had been here before us, Stan. I found a rusty, dull-edged trowel and tossed my spoon away.

I worked my hands through all of this. I told myself that I'd uncover, grow and gather, separate and trim. And that the watch I'd keep would be a tighter one.

I work so hard. But it takes so long. Every day I watch but I never actually see anything grow. I know something's down there; I've seen before. And I can't imagine that just one or two little instances of tearing up the wrong thing would mean that nothing will come back. But the ones that are here are really wimpy. Every puny blade cowers at rain and blushes at sun and trembles when I come near it with my trowel. I wish you were here to convince me, Stan. But I don't know where you are. Did you return to the monastery? The stories you told me of where you had spent the years before our reunion were so spare and stark and lean, so full of your denials.

I work so hard. I get so bored. But what else would I do? Shuffle back to the kitchen, sit at the three-legged card table (I've propped it up with a pile of old newspapers), stare out of the broken window watching the clouds rearrange themselves, and play solitaire? I wish the garden could be like a movie, Stan, one of those terrifically nurdy educational filmstrips we saw when we were kids. Time-lapse nature photography so we could just sit back and watch the action unfold. Stems shooting up and buds zipping open and perfect petals popping into bloom in living colour. And in a time frame we could understand easily. I liked it when we didn't have to wait around forever for history to happen, and when we knew, with certainty, what would occur. They were reliable stories in biology class. They told us how it ought to be, then showed us that it was. Did we ever see a movie in biology class that showed a flower opening to a rotten, pocked inside? I don't remember one.

But, Stan, I wait so long and I think, oh god, it's not going to happen, it's never going to happen again, oh god, and I want to give up and I almost give up.

But then I'm teased. It teases me on the back of my neck. It coaxes me off my aching knees and I stretch my face to the cold slit of light in the heavens.

Stan, come back. You'll love the firm stalks, the warm, moist bowers of shade, the clean, fine lines of the trellis. Oh dear, Stan, I – I'm – stretching the truth, and we cared so much about the truth before. But it isn't quite as lovely as I said. Sure there's stuff growing, hardy rough stuff. Briars. Dandelions. But there isn't much that anyone would want. I want to weed, but I'm afraid of what I might pull up. Like a dart gun. Or a flashlight. Or a bit of a coloured rag.

My ragged clothes are all the same generic bag-lady, one-colour-fits-all grey-brown colour. My skin too. My hi-tops are falling apart, holes in the soles and holes in the toes and heels. My hands are rough and my stubby, filthy fingernails poke out of my torn canvas garden gloves. I consider the term 'Mother Nature' offensive.

I stick my hand in my pocket and touch the grungy cloth. I remember my hand around the smooth wooden flagpole and lifting my face to the dawn-coloured colours flying. I twist my neck down to look back at the broken glass of our bedroom window. Then, beside that, to the scuff marks by the door. The white walls of our home, your fine spare design, dear Stan, is splattered with mud.

I pull myself around on my knees. I try to turn broken eggshells, apple cores and ends of loaves of bread back into the ground. But there's other stuff I can't bury deep enough. Should I tell you, Stan? A little tennis shoe, a worn felt hat, a spoke.

It isn't that we wanted to be arrogant. We were as innocent as kids. We thought we had discovered something clean and plain and simple and good. And obvious. Why hadn't somebody thought of this way out before? We needed one, Stan. We clapped our hands like babies playing patticake. Then we went at it.

Perhaps we should have known, dear Stan. We had, after all, been raised on the story of them. It was a story with a moral, the only one that both the history books agreed on. That everyone, no matter how small or young or odd could – no – ought, to be like them. Everyone. Even us, dear Stan. Especially us. There were black-and-white line drawings of them in books, authentic reconstructions of period houses and furniture and authentic dress. Perhaps this is from whence your interest in interior design and fashion dates.

We saw filmstrips about them in history class. Presided over by a bent, thin, bespectacled hawk of a woman, Miss Hardison, whose dyed black hair barely covered the hearing aid she tried to conceal behind her left ear, we were instructed in their goodly ways. Miss Hardison would clap her long, thin-fingered hands – no wedding ring, we noticed with a snicker – and wait for us to be silent. She'd firmly remind us, again, that if any acting up occurred, she would have no choice but to turn the lights back on immediately and make us read the entire rest of the period, and we would forego our privilege – not our right – to ever see films in class again. We'd sit bolt upright in our straightback wood and metal desks, slap our hands together and try to stifle our giggles. This was always easier for you than for me, dear Stan. You were a good boy, well-behaved, polite and always clean. While I was rude, unruly as my short cropped hair, foul-mouthed, skin-kneed and blue-and-purple-fingered from where I had drawn a skull-and-crossbones tattoo on my hand.

Miss Hardison would ask the row leaders to walk – quietly, she'd emphasize with a hiss – to their respective windows, and pull the blinds. After they had done so and returned to their seats – quietly, though usually with at least one irrepressible tremble of a shoulder – Miss Hardison would lift herself from her chair and stand stiff and thin with her back to the blackboard on which she'd written the name of the movie and a couple of dates from history. She'd squint out over the room with her hawk eyes, purse her thin white lips into a beak and slowly shake her head as she regarded the sorry crew of us junior delinquents in training. Then suddenly, sharply, she'd sniff, twitch her left eyebrow up into a peak and announce, with horrible finality, 'Stephen Matthews!' Then this sweet, shy, pale boy, the one who'd been the quietest during her predatory glare at us, would try to shrink into his desk.'Stephen Matthews!' she'd repeat. ('Nicholas Wilson', 'Andrew Johnson', 'Stanley—' Sometimes it was you, dear Stan—), 'You will kindly shut off the lights while I prepare the projector.' Then this quiet, pale, shy boy – it was you, Stanley, some- times – would shuffle, head bowed, embarrassed to have been caught being such a model student again, and slink over to the light switch by the door. Miss Hardison would march – she could have balanced the entire sixth-grade fiction library on her head with her absolutely swingless walk – to the back of the class where the library assistant, a pasty-faced boy with premature acne, had set up the projector and a straight-backed chair for her. Miss Hardison tucked her grey pleated skirt neatly beneath her slender hips and sat down. She straightened her shoulders, placed her left hand carefully on the start lever of the projector and announced, more loudly than she needed to, 'Be careful not to trip in the dark on the way back to your chair, Stephen' (Nicholas, Andrew, Stanley—). Then, 'You may shut off the lights now, Stephen.' We'd hear the click as Steve cut the lights, then the click of the projector's switch. We'd giggle when we were plunged into the semi-dark. Immediately, Miss Hardison would snap, 'Children!' to make us think she'd heard us. Then we'd hear the warped, slow, then too fast, too loud opening bars of the vaguely orchestral, ridiculously enthusiastic theme tune of Scholastic Services Film Service, Inc. The logo of which, a fat beige diamond on a maroon rectangle with the name in plain block letters underneath, would appear as soon as Miss Hardison quit fiddling with the focus. The music, if you were generous enough to call the bubble gum Boston Pops march ditty music, started out in a loopy cattawampus rhythm: it sounded the way you looked in the Homecoming Fair Fun House Mirror. Miss Hardison would always gasp at the assault of noise when the opening bars screeched at us. She'd turn the volume down so far we'd miss the first part of the narration. She'd yell nervously above the words, 'Can everybody hear? Can everybody hear? Raise your hand if you can't hear the film properly.' And sometimes someone in the back row, right in front of her, sometimes me, would raise their hand, my purple smudged tattoo, for fun, so she'd turn the sound back up full blast.

After the music died, a boring man's voice came on. The narrator was always a man and he always spoke too slowly, as if we were stupid, and he awkwardly emphasized the wrong words in the wrong sentences. We never understood his enthusiasms. The screen showed a poorly executed map of Europe: aqua-blue seas and white-yellow outlines of green countries so small we couldn't distinguish them. Then a big light-purple arrow sprung out of France or Germany, or whatever their names were then, and stretched down the continent. Its sharp point turned, about Italy, to its left, our right, towards the Middle East. The pointed lavender tip of the arrow always stopped just before it got to the edge of the frame; we never saw how it ended. As the impossibly pleasant narrator told us about how small communities, hearing of the noble march, gave, or rather, lost, their own to the cause, the flickering screen showed smaller arrows, also dawn-coloured, feeding into the bigger one. Like streams into a river. Like a filmstrip we'd seen in biology class. Then, as we were wondering when the arrow was going to end, the cartoon map blurred like ink to navy blue. Then black. The room was dark. We couldn't see the screen on the wall. It stayed dark a couple of terrible seconds.

You and I stared, dear Stan, at the terrible dark, while our better behaved classmates took advantage of the break to scribble their history notes. But you and I were wondering, Stan, what happened to the arrow, what happened in the dark we couldn't see.

But we didn't find out. Because then the screen on the wall began to lighten. At first weak, like the pale beam of a tiny flashlight was on it, then it broke into blobs of colour, then focused into shapes we were familiar with. And then we saw the children.

At first we laughed at them, the boys with their ludicrous Little Lord Fauntleroy haircuts and prissy leotards and too-short shorts and ballet slippers, the girls wearing tall pink conehead hats with scarves that hung from them like towels. They marched along like dolls, obedient to the unbelievably rousing narration. We were embarrassed for our fellow kids, for how they had to dress like nurds to satisfy the obviously adult directors and writers of history. We knew – we weren't born yesterday – what went into this careful propaganda. We watched the goody-two-shoes march behind their pastel banner, their liquid eyes gazing heavenwards, while a little ray of sunshine shone down on them. We watched big kids put their arms around little kids' shoulders, and, thumb-sucking babies sit in older siblings' arms. But we knew the truth of these relationships. In real life we all tried our damnedest to avoid our brothers and sisters at recess, on the bus, in the market place.

The film showed the children marching to somewhere their parents had failed to get before. We laughed at the incredibly noble sentiments the movie-makers tried to instill in us. We looked around in the semi-dark of the room, searching for the faces of the secret, select minority of our compatriots to whom we'd flash our smirking imitation of the pony league piety of the on-screen kids. We weren't about to march off to the Holy Lands, much less to Delaware or Kansas, to reclaim possession of the chilly First Methodist basement.

What we might have done, however, and this was the hook that kept us quiet in our desks in the darkened room, was run away. Because we knew, in the secret code of kids adults forget, what the child crusaders were really up to. They secretly told us in code, in the special way they held their wrists, the blue and purple smudges on their hands, that they were a tough, rebellious band of runaways. The movie kids winked at us kids with the mark in a way that neither Miss Hardison, nor the naive narrator, nor our boring regular classmates who wanted to grow up, could see. The kid crusaders weren't marching to redeem a has-been plot of real estate; they'd simply, suddenly, in the dark when their moms and dads weren't looking, flipped their parents off and hit the road.

We loved to think of the wandering kids of yore as a gang like us, or like we hoped to be, unfettered by our parents, school, or anyone to tell us how to be. We didn't want to come home before dark. Or ever. We resented our parents' sly stage whispers, 'Just wait ...' or 'Someday, kid, you'll see ...' their sinister benevolence, their condescending tolerance, their arrogant assumption they knew best for us, that we were just a stage that we'd go through. Because we were a different species, Stan, unlike they'd ever been. We were going to run away, for real, and live on nuts and berries, or marshmallows and pizza and cokes. We'd wear blue jeans and tennis shoes every day and make a bonfire of our Sunday best and our stupid raincoats. We'd share ice-cream-and-pancake breakfasts with our dogs and we would never, ever, wash a dish or make a bed or take out the garbage again. To these pure dreams of us, dear Stan, we would be true.

And we had evidence of who we were. For we carried, in the pockets of our elastic waist-band shorts, along with our marbles and pieces of strings, our plastic army men and thumb-printed, half-chewed wads of Bazooka gum, our dawn-coloured banner. This was the sign by which we'd lead each other out on our crusade.

We sat in the dark of Miss Hardison's room hearing, without listening to the rattle of the projector, the rustle of our cut-and paste projects on the wall, the squeak of our neighbours' chairs. Sometimes when the soundtrack of the film garbled, we would hear the flapping of the flag and the tramping of a million pairs of fellow gangsters' tennis shoes as we all marched, unchaperoned and free. Sometimes, the movie frames got dark, pock-marked with caramel-coloured brown where the film had been burnt in previous careless showings. We filled these gaps with pictures of ourselves leading our special class-mates, then special kids from other schools, then different states and countries, like Japan. We knew that we were everywhere, and we also knew that there were kids like us who didn't know they were, who'd had it squelched, but that when they saw our colours, they would recognize and join our true crusade.

What happened in the dark when we weren't looking, Stan? All of the sudden the lights came on. All of the sudden Miss Hardison was giving us a pop quiz on names and dates we hadn't learned, and grilling us about what we'd been doing when we should have been paying attention. All of the sudden we needed to make excuses for ourselves and hide our secret crusade.

All of the sudden we'd outgrown our desks and were fiddling around in the pockets of our full-length trousers hoping we hadn't lost our coloured cloth. And all of the sudden, the Bruces and Mikes, not the sweet, shy boys who were called on to switch off the lights, had settled down with the cute, polite girls in the class, and moved to garden houses in Vermont.

An alternative was imperative. Miss Hardison and the nameless, vanilla-voiced man who had grilled us with the story of the Holy Wars were calling our alternative unnatural, like trying to fit the slipper on the Prince's foot, like having the young leave the dying. But they were the ones who were wrong, right Stan?

But what we didn't know, dear Stan, that special day much later, after you and I had met again, the day we looked each other in the eye and vowed our truth through sickness and through health, through snow and rain, through our crusade, 'til love do us part, that it wouldn't be love that parted us.

What happened in the dark when we weren't looking, Stan? Sure we closed our eyes, but only for a couple of blissful moments. I remember the way you held your head, the sweet lithe way of your wrists, the shadow of the dawn-coloured flag we wed one another beneath.

We were kids, Stan. Could we be faulted for wanting what we couldn't have, for doing the thing that we did naturally? Could we have known our coupling could get us this? Is isn't what we bore, but what surrounded it. Something older and meaner and, yes, something bigger than both of us.

Oh dear, sweet, understanding, dear forgiving Stan. What I told you about the garden? Was a lie. I'd never lied to you before, dear Stan, not yet. But lies are the only thing that keep me going anymore. Because the truth is, I'm in a rock heap. I work hard but I can't move anything. And we couldn't move it together even if you were here. The blocks are heavier than they ought to be. I can't see to the tops, but they weigh as if something is perched on them.

I'm kneeling here at work. I'm trying to build a humble, quiet niche for both of us. Come back, please Stan. I promise, every stab I make in this hard ground, that we'll behave. We'll hold each other's arms while we shuffle through the rocks. I'll overcook your vegetables and darn your socks. I'll read you the morning paper while you doze with your slippers and pipe.

But who believes me? Even the dirt knows that my recent mumblings and wringing of my hands are not sincere. That had I strength or hope or something firm, or something from the time when we were kids, I would be kicking and screaming and tearing them up, then tearing them out; I would crusade.

But I am broken.

Stan, I know I'm bad and selfish to wish you back to this crappy place; I'm sorry. But I simply don't want to get what I am going to get alone.

They think I haven't seen them snooping around in the shadows of rubble, fingering through the papers we hid in the mattress, the rolled-up bills in the coffee can under the sink. They thought I'd get lulled into thinking I was safe because who'd want a broken, rocky lot where nothing grows? But I've seen them on these piss-poor heaven drizzling nights or days. I can no longer tell the difference. I've seen the little heiresses and heirs scurrying around with their tape measures and their surveyors' kits, their blueprints for selling off parcels of us. I know their greedy mouths, their sucking lips, their sticky hands they rub in anticipation.

I remember something else about that movie, Stan. That in those days the kids of faith paraded Europe, in those middle days of faith in dark, the days when they knew just how many days there were until the final one, that it was everywhere. It wasn't a surprise, dear Stan, did not discriminate. Did the kids of yore crusading for a higher love know secretly, more secretly than we, that however far they tried to go, whatever old fogies they tried to leave, that their crusade would not take them away from it? But did the kids decide to march off anyway, to see a bit of the world and have a gay old time before they got it: No one ever told us how the children's crusade ended, Stan. And as ten- or twelve-year-olds we didn't wonder what became of them, whether they were sold as slaves or grew up into bureaucrats or *nouveau* gentry in Vermont, or stumbled home to find that, somehow in the dark when they weren't looking, something of an epidemic size had orphaned them.

As kids we loved unthinkingly the gory details of that safely distant age. Those of us with sloppy tattoo-ed purple hands drew lots to see who got to do the in-class oral report on it. We loved the shocked, horrified looks on our squeamish classmates' faces when we gleefully and brazenly showed them pictures from medical books before Miss Hardison put a stop to this quite unnecessary display of blue and purple marks on skin.

You'd get the marks and you'd be gone in three days time. Or it could linger and you'd decay for ages. At first they thought that they could run from it, from city to country, but it followed them. They thought the poison air had carried it, or rays of sun. Once your mark was discovered, you tried to hide. They'd mark your house, they'd shut you in, they'd blame you, dump you in a cart. Then they would leave.

Should we have noticed when we started losing at Ring Around the Rosie? When they covered their noses and ran away and snickered god bless you when we thought we only had hay fever? Was it our fault we didn't ask them why they started to carry oranges and cloves when they were forced to go on family outings with us? When they made us wear those jingling bells so they could hear us coming and run away?

But Stan, we had been warned: what we did to our parents, and their failure to recapture what was lost.

It was a terrible day, dear Stan, when you and I cowered in our trembling home and when you put your sweet head to my breast and sobbed and when I held you and rocked you and told you to run and that I'd join you again in a couple of days. You lifted your sweet face up to me and asked me, 'Why are they leaving?'

I didn't answer you.

I'd worked so hard. I work so hard. I try to do things right but it's so hard. It's useless to water the cracks. But I work and work and I think, oh god, it isn't going to happen. I want to give up. I start to give up. But then a little ray of sunshine breaks on my neck.

Only it's not a ray of sunshine.

It's the middle of a stormy night. It's a searchlight, spearing down on my neck from the top of the trellis. I scurry like a rat into a crack of the rock, hold my breath, and hope the high beam doesn't glint against my trusty metal trowel. After a few seconds, I peek my wet-streaked, dirty face out from behind my cover of rock. I look up to the top of the thin white trellis and I see little black birds on it, murmuring like doves – no - giggling. I look back to the house to see, as much as I can on this moonless night, if they are there as well, but I can't see. But I feel the light tickling on the back of my neck again and I spin to look back at the trellis. It isn't birds; it's hands. The flashlight is one of the cute bright lavender ones we got for the children that Christmas so in case they ever got lost in the dark they could find us. I close my eyes and shudder to think whose cold yellow light has discovered me.

In an instant, it's as light as a rainless afternoon. And the terrible children are streaming, bursting, clambering over the top of the shaky trellis and back into my little patch of rubble. Perhaps I should have built a wall around these scraps. But I didn't want to. For the same reasons we didn't want to when we first made this house our nest, because we wanted to believe and act and live the way we were, on the border but in touch, and open, generous and without lies. Only now do I see that our chatter of equality, of each one to one's own, was arrogance. We were ambitious fools to think we could be different just because we were. As if no kids had ever thought they could escape before.

I didn't learn. The first time or the next. I wanted to build a trellis this time, a light, thin thing from whence to prop a garden. Or our colours, Stan.

But the children have been drawn to it. They think they've read a secret sign and they have come to have it. I hear the snap of the trellis' baby-like bones and I see the white frame collapse. I hear the whup of a billow of cloth. A line of kids are teetering on the trellis' upper bar. They giggle and dance then leap off as it falls towards the hard, grey ground. The children run a ring around me, singing the awful ditty I recognize, about me being something that's not grown here, that I'll fall, and that they'll scatter ashes over me. I hear the pitter-patter of little feet as they goose-step in their round, rubber-toed tennis shoes. They've got their flashlights and their electric saw, their jackhammers. Some of them drag a cart.

They scramble over the rocks as easily as monkeys. It doesn't take long for them to bash what I've been working so hard at for ages. They're aiming the saw at the legs of the trellis. I don't want to see it, Stan, but I remember your horrible loss. I cover my face with my hands. I hear the bottom of the trellis collapse into the rubble. And then I can see, outside, the place I tried so hard to live without. My small grey lot is an island in a big black avenue. The avenue is lined on each side by densely packed, shade-giving – the brightness of the children's lights has made me see in spots – trees? And I feel, suddenly, as soft as fingers, as soft as skin, the drop of tiny petals, of dogwood and cherry blossoms soothing my pockmarked skin. I tremble to think these trees have grown without my seeing them, almost in reach, beyond the trellis I was so intent upon, and that the children, bless their hearts, have come back, despite their overly rambunctious style, to show me, a runny-eyed old hag, what my hard work has yielded. I put my dirty wet-streaked face in my hands and fall to the ground, my butt on my heels, and lift my hands to the heavens and thank them. I hear, as though it were an answer from the heavens, a gentle breeze. The breeze lifts my matted hair from the back of my neck and blows cool breath on my skin. Then the breeze gets loud, not answering me, but telling me. It's wind, a storm, louder, closer than weather. I blink the spots from my eyes and see it isn't petals on my blotted skin, but confetti, and the sound isn't wind, but voices. The sun is blocked, not by an avenue of trees, but by a hankie-waving multitude. The children have come back in a grand parade, a victory parade.

The people lining both sides of the street feel pride and pity for the marvellous kids whose faces look like pseudo-urchins. I bet they use a make-up artist. They look like child saints, not the nasty knee-high hoods we know they are. The calculating kids are singing their playground chant of an anthem. I watch the eyes of the crowd water when the children stumble, adorably, over the words too big for them, then stumble, one-legged, on their pint-sized crutches and under the weight of their bright, dawn-coloured banner. Only I know that as soon as they had trampled my lot they had tied one of their ankles beneath their too-long shirts, that their lameness is a temporary play for sympathy, that the colours they fly are stolen. They limp along with their arms in little slings passing out leaflets and sponsorship applications and tax-free contribution forms. Wouldn't we like to support them? Couldn't we sign their pledge cards? Wouldn't we like to open our hearts to them? No, we wouldn't, thank you very much, not you and me, Stan. Because we already have. And the monstrous little shits have cleaned us out. Of our hearts and our homes and our lives and both our cheque books. And now this final pissing excuse for a garden.

The whole damned foolish avenue is emptying their pockets and their pants for the terrible kids. I want to warn them. No, that's not true. I don't give a fuck about those idiots if they are fool enough to throw themselves away on a few pretty faces. Look at the children's teeth, for god's sake. Have I not warned enough by my example? No, what I wish is that I could undo what the little bloodsuckers did to us. I wish that what is happening to me – again – would not.

The children run a ring around me, Stan. Their pretty eyes look up at me. The clapping public on the street can see the childrens' upward gaze. They think it's towards the colours, then past, to the heavens. But the kids are leering up at me. Their grubby hands are grabbing me. Their greedy mouths are open and they've got me by my tits and skin and eyes. My darling babes are murmuring, like joy, the lie I taught them: *'I love you. I'll never leave.'*

I open my mouth to beg them to quit, to pity a poor old woman and let me go. But they stop my mouth with kisses. Then they knock me on the back of my neck. I fall forward on my hands and knees. They climb up on to my stooped old-woman back and make me carry them. They wave parade waves to the crowd. I try to fall, but the littlest ones are holding me down by my knees.

After they tire of riding me, they leap off my back and snap me up straight by my shoulders, cracking my crooked back. They stick what feels like a flag-pole in my hand – the kids do this to spite us, Stan – then something thin and metal in my other hand. They shove me back to the end of the crusade. I shuffle behind them, my mousy thin hair in a scarf, my long, black, ratty skirt sagging to my ankles. They've replaced my fingerless gardening gloves with rubber ones. My hands feel moist and slippery inside them. My hollow cheeks are sucked in tight. I try to curse the children, but I'm toothless. I can't even spit. I clutch my gnarled fingers around what they've placed in my hands – a mop and pail.

They've stationed a couple of pygmy toughs in oversized trench-coats on my tail. Their beardless faces glare at me from beneath the brims of their *film noir* gangster hats. They shove their pudgy chocolate-covered hands into their pockets, then stick their hard bulging coats into my ribs and backside. I hope they don't have real guns. But on the other hand, I hope they do; I'd feel ridiculous if I was being strong-armed by a couple of squirt toys. They slip along beside me, touching me and nudging me and hovering in my skirts where the hankie-waving crowd won't see them. The people on the avenue, the generation you and I grew up with, Stan, don't notice the dripping shit the children shit. Or that I shuffle along behind the children, slopping it into my charwoman's pail of slop.

Why didn't we, Stan, when we could have, call a halt to the fools' crusade, held their pelican heads down in the bath, or told them to play in the traffic or with the candy-like capsules in the medicine cabinet? Why didn't we, Stan? Or if we couldn't do that, why didn't we axe ourselves and beat the rush? We knew exactly what was going to happen. The writing was on the wall, on the film screen in front of class. What made us look away from the one true terrible truth we ever learned? That love is that which tears the heart, which tears the body from the heart.

What made us look away, dear Stan, what made us blind, was the one true terrible thing that we desired: the pretty babies of our dreams. Whom we conceived in violence and bore in blood. Who tore themselves away from us. Who left. Who leave, but leave enough of them inside of us to keep on coming back to tear us up again.

Dear Stanley, husband of my heart, I need to warn you.

Will one of the children be our messenger for old time's sake? I doubt the kids will mind me, but maybe they'll do it for something – a home-cooked meal, a tit to suck, advance on their allowance, the keys to the car, a hand job, a blow, though they need nothing I have left to take. But I need to send you a message and I can't move. But the children can. They're leading the crusade. You'll hear the ripples of our colours, Stan, and the pitter and patter and goose step of little feet. But Stanley, when you get this message, run. I know you can't see where you're going, but run. Though they'll outrun you. Even if they slow their pace, they will catch up with you.

Stan, the kids are slowing their pace. They're hanging their heads and drooping their lips and sniffing and wiping their eyes in the worst child-star exaggeration of crying. And they're telling the crowds, in the ultimate sympathy-grabbing ploy, the one this whole charade has led up to, that they are all alone. Like wee little lambs. That they are orphans, Stan. That they've been left by us.

Stan, you and I are the only ones who know, but we know well enough, just how the children desecrate, they mutilate what's thicker than water and thicker than love, with their lie. Only you know and I know, my doddering groom, that the babies are without their loving parents because they left us.

But who'll believe us, Stan? We can tell the truth until we're blue in the face and purple and blue in the hands, but who'll believe us?

No one ever told us how the children's crusade ended, Stan.

*

But I'll tell you.

It ended that day when we cowered and knelt in the home we had inherited. You put your sweet head to my breast and sobbed and said you didn't want to see. I covered your eyes and I told you to run and I would follow after you in a while. Then I covered your ears and I yelled at our terrible children. I yelled at them: *Don't be like them.* I yelled at them to leave and not come back.

I lied when I yelled at the children. I lied because I wanted them to see the terrible thing they'd done and to say that they wouldn't again. I said I did, but I didn't want them to leave. I wanted them to stay, and if they couldn't, at least to pity me with a child's lie. Though I knew then, though I denied I did, that no one ever changes, neither the children, from any age, nor you, nor I. And that the children won't come back and be the kids we wanted so unbearably.

And that I never could work hard enough in this pitiful empty lot to grow anything that could cover the terrible loathing, the terrible love I bear them.

I lag at the back of the children's crusade. I'm tired and the pail they make me carry weighs me down. One of the pygmy toughs beside me sticks the toe of its little tennie out to trip me. I see what it's doing, but I can't stop myself from falling, knees first, then face down, into the dirt. The little tough presses its sneaker on the back of my neck. I can't get up, but I lift my head a bit and see, shoe-level, the soles of a thousand rubber-toed hi-tops and hundreds of fake little crutches. I'm grateful I'm here at the end of the march so there aren't any kids behind me to goose step over me. I drop my face in the dirt again. If anyone on the avenue could see me, they might take me for dead. But the kids don't. The little tough takes its foot off my neck, squats down and sticks, right up to my dirty wet-streaked face, its bright, pretty sparkling eyes. I open my mouth to try to beg it to leave me alone. Assured that I'll survive until their next tramp back to me, it leaps up and scampers off.

I kneel up slowly. The dirt is up and over my legs, I lift my dirty wet-streaked face to see the marching line of them shrink towards the horizon. I see above the border wall – morning sky? – the banner we flew? – our dawn-coloured colours, Stan.

Dear Stanley, if the kids come back, I know they will, for good this time, they won't, but if they do, if they come back and stop the march and say that they are sorry, that they've finally learnt, and that they'll stay, I know, if there is anything I've taught the kids, that whatever they tell me, however they look, however they say they've changed, that they are lying. But Stanley, if the children toddle back to me on their tiny toes and their chubby darling legs, if they come back with their pink-as-petals fingers and their sparkling eyes, their baby teeth, I'll welcome them. And though I won't, I'll tell them I believe them when they nuzzle me and gurgle in their baby talk that they won't leave – again – or leave, and raise their eager mouths and say the terrible, terrible lie that I want them to tell me.

In AD 1212 . . .

. . . an orphan shepherd boy had a vision of Christ in the hills near Cloyes, in the Vendôme region of France. Dressed as a poor pilgrim, Christ told the young Stephen that he had been chosen to lead the next Crusade to the Holy Land. He explained to the boy that since 1095, when Pope Urban II had first exhorted Christians to recover Jerusalem, the adults had failed: now the children would have their chance.

Stephen set out for Paris in April of 1212. By the time he stood before King Philip of France, he was the acknowledged leader of a large troop. The King, however, was not prepared to listen seriously to Stephen's proposal to equip, mount, arm and finance an army of six- to thirteen-year-old crusaders. But instead of returning home – he had none to return to – Stephen set out to recruit his army from all over France. By June he was on his way to the port of Marseilles in command of 30,000 children.

In the same year, another boy not yet in his teens raised 40,000 children in Germany. Nicholas of Cologne lead his army across the Alps to gain papal sanction for his crusade to convert the Turks through Faith rather than battle. Pope Innocent III ordered the children home – and like Stephen, they ignored him. It is not known whether the French and German children's crusades arose spontaneously, or whether they were co-ordinated. What is clear, is that both boys – the orphan, and the son of a wealthy man – were ready to try and change the world torn apart by their elders.

Many adults recorded being deeply moved by the children's march: they believed in the children's devotion, and fed and cared for them as they travelled. But unlike the papally authorized crusades, there are no surviving memoirs of participants, and no one knows what happened to either Stephen, Nicholas or the thousands of children that followed them.

ABOUT THE AUTHOR

Rebecca Brown's previous novel, *The Haunted House,* was published by Seal Press in 1990. Her other works include *The Terrible Girls* (Picador) and a short story collection, *The Evolution of Darkness* (Brilliance Books); she also appears in the fiction collection *Mae West is Dead* (Faber). She lives in Seattle, Washington.